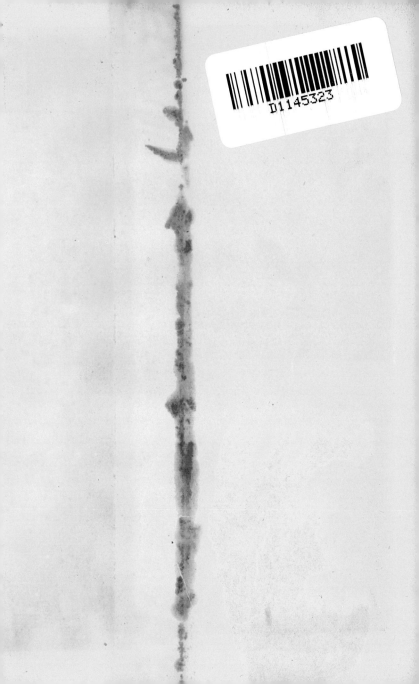

THE UPAS TREE

To
V. C. B.

THE UPAS TREE

By

FLORENCE L. BARCLAY

Author of "The Rosary," etc.

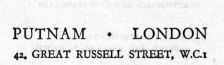

PUTNAM • LONDON
42, GREAT RUSSELL STREET, W.C.1

MADE IN GREAT BRITAIN

122nd Thousand

BOOK
PRODUCTION
WAR ECONOMY
STANDARD

THIS BOOK IS PRODUCED IN
COMPLETE CONFORMITY WITH THE
AUTHORISED ECONOMY STANDARDS

PRINTED BY
JARROLD AND SONS LTD. NORWICH

CONTENTS

CONTENTS

PART I

CHAPTER I

WHICH SHALL SPEAK FIRST?

RONALD WEST stood at the window of his wife's sitting-room, looking across the bright garden-borders to the wide park beyond, and wondering how on earth he should open the subject of which his mind had been full during their morning ride.

He had swung off his own horse a few moments before; thrown the bridle to a waiting groom, and made his way round to her stirrup. Then he had laid his hand upon Silverheels' mane, and looking up into his wife's glowing, handsome face, he had said: "May I come to your room for a talk, Helen? I have something very important to tell you."

Helen had smiled down upon him.

"I thought my cavalier was miles away from his horse and his wife, during most of the ride. But, if he proposes taking me on the same distant journey, he shall be forgiven. Also, I have something to tell *you*, Ronnie, and I see the turret clock gives us an hour before luncheon. I must scribble out a message for the village; then I will come to you at once, without stopping to change."

She laid her hand on his shoulder, and dropped lightly to the ground. Then, telling the groom to wait, she passed into the hall.

Ronald left her standing at the table, walked into the sitting-room alone, and suddenly realised that when you have thought of a thing continuously, day and night, during the best part of a week, and kept it to yourself, it is not easy to begin explaining it to another person—even though that other person be your always kind, always understanding, altogether perfect wife!

He had forgotten to leave his hat and gloves in the hall. He now tossed them into a chair—Helen's own particular chair it so happened—but kept his riding-crop in his hand, and thwacked his leather gaiters with it, as he stood in the bay window.

It was such a perfect spring morning! The sun shone in through the old-fashioned lattice panes.

Some silly old person of a bygone century had scratched with a diamond on one of these a rough cross, and beneath it the motto: *In hoc vince*.

Ronald had inveighed against this. If Helen's old ancestor, having nothing better to do, had wanted to write down a Latin motto, he should have put it in his pocket-book, or, better still, on the even more transitory pages of the blotter, instead of scribbling on the beautiful diamond panes of the old Grange windows. But Helen had laughed and said: "I should think he lived before the time of blotters, dear! No doubt the morning sun was shining on the glass, Ronnie, as he stood at the window. It was of the cross gleaming in the sunlight, that he wrote: *In this conquer*. If we could but remember it, the path of self-sacrifice and clear shining is always the way to victory."

Helen invariably stood up for her ancestors, which was annoying to a very modern young man who, not being aware of possessing any, considered ancestors unnecessary and obsolete.

But to-day the glittering letters shone out to him as an omen.

He meant to conquer, in this, as in all else.

It was curious that Helen should have chanced upon the simile of a distant journey. Another good omen! *In hoc vince!*

He heard her coming.

Now—how should he begin? He must be very tactful. He must break it to her gently.

Helen, closing the door behind her, came slowly down the sunny room. The graceful lines of her tall figure looked well, in the severe simplicity of her riding-habit. Her mass of beautiful hair was tucked away beneath her riding-hat. But nothing could take from the calm sweetness of her face, nor the steady expectant kindness of her eyes. Helen's eyes always looked out upon the world, as if they expected to behold a Vision Beautiful.

As she moved towards the bay window, she was considering whether she would decide to have her say first, or whether she would let Ronnie begin. Her wonderful news was so all-important. Having made up her mind that the time had come when she might at last share it with Ronnie, it seemed almost impossible to wait one moment before telling him. On the other hand, it would be so absorbing to them both, that probably Ronnie's subject would be allowed to lapse, completely forgotten and unmentioned. Nothing which was of even the most transitory interest to Ronnie, ever met this fate at his wife's hands. Therefore the very certainty that her news would outweigh his, inclined her to let him speak first.

She was spared the responsibility of decision.

Ronald, turning quickly, faced his wife. Hesitation seemed futile; promptness, essential. *In hoc vince!*

"Helen," he said, "I want to go to Central Africa."

Helen looked at him in silence, during a moment of immense astonishment.

Then she lifted his hat and gloves, laid them upon a table, seated herself in her easy-chair, and carefully flicked some specks of dust from her riding-habit.

"That is a long way to want to go, darling," she said, quietly. "But I can see you think something of imperative importance is calling you there. Sit down and tell me all about it, right from the beginning. It is a far cry, from our happy, beautiful life here, to Central Africa. You have jumped me to the goal, without any knowledge of the way. Now suppose you take me gently along your mental route."

Ronald flung himself, with a sigh of relief, into the deep basket-work chair opposite Helen's. His boyish face cleared visibly; then brightened into enthusiasm. He stretched out his legs, put his hands behind his head, and looked admiringly across at his wife.

"Helen, you are so perfectly splendid in always understanding, always making it quite easy for a fellow to tell you things. You have a way of looking past all minor details, straight to the great essentials. Most women would stand——"

"Never mind what most women would do, Ronnie. I never stand, if I can sit down! It is a waste of useful energy. But you must tell me 'the great essentials,' as they appear to you, if I am to view them properly. Why do you want to go to Central Africa?"

Ronald leapt up and stood with his back to the mantelpiece.

"Helen, I have a new plot; a quite wonderful love-story; better than anything I have done yet. But the scene is laid in Central Africa, and I must go out there to get the setting vivid and correct. You remember how thrilled we were the other day, by the account of that missionary chap, who disappeared into the long grass, thirteen feet high, over twenty years ago; lived and worked among the natives, cut off from all civilisation; then, at last, crawled out again and saw a railway train for the first time in twenty-three years; got on board, and came home, full of wonderful tales of his experiences? Well—you know how, after he had been out there a few years, he found he desperately needed a wife; remembered a plucky girl he had known when he was a boy in England, and managed to get a letter home, asking her to come out to him? She came, and safely reached the place appointed, at the fringe of the wild growth. There she waited several months. But at last the man who had called to her in his need, crawled out of the long grass, took her to himself, and they crawled in again—man and wife—and were seen no more, until they reappeared many years later. Well—that true story has given me the idea of a plot, which will, I verily believe, take the world by storm! So original and thrilling! Far beyond any missionary love-stories."

Helen's calm eyes looked into the excited shining of his.

"Dear, why shouldn't a missionary's love-story be as exciting as any other? I don't quite see how you can better the strangely enthralling tale to which we listened."

"Ah, don't you?" cried Ronald West. "That's because you are not a writer of romances! My dear girl, *two* men crawled out of the long grass thirteen feet high, at the place where the woman was waiting! Two men—do you see? And the man who crawled out first was *not* the man who had sent for her! *He* turned up just too late. Now, do you see?"

"I see," said Helen. "Thirteen is always apt to be an unlucky number."

"Oh, don't joke!" cried Ronald. "I haven't time to tell you, now, how it all works out. But it's quite the strongest thing I've thought of yet. And do you see what it means to me? Think of the weird, mysterious atmosphere of Central Africa, as a setting for a really strong love-interest. Imagine three quite modern, present-day people, learning to know their own hearts and each other's, fighting out the crisis of their lives according to the accepted rules and standards of twentieth-century civilisation—yet all amongst the wild primitive savagery of uncivilised tribes, and the extraordinary primeval growths of the unexplored jungles, where plants ape animals, and animals ape men, and all nature rears its head with a loose rein, as if defying method,

law, order and construction! Why, merely to walk through
some of the tropical houses at Kew gives one a sort of law-
less feeling! If I stay long among the queer gnarled plants
—all spiky and speckled and hairy; squatting, plump and
ungainly on the ground, or spreading huge knotted arms
far overhead, as if reaching out for things they never visibly
attain—I always emerge into the ordinary English atmosphere outside, feeling altogether unconventional. As I
walk across the well-kept lawns, I find it almost difficult to
behave with decorum. It takes me quite a long time to
become really commonplace and conventional once more."

Helen smiled. "Darling," she said, "I think you must
have visited the tropical plants in Kew Gardens more
frequently than I realised! I shall have to forbid Kew, when
certain important County functions are pending."

"Oh, bother the County!" cried Ronnie. "I never went
in for a French dancing-master to bid me mind my P's and
Q's! But, seriously, Helen, don't you understand how
much this means to me? Both my last novels have had
tame English settings. I can't go on for ever letting my
people make love in well-kept gardens!"

"Dear Ronnie, you have a good precedent. The first
couple on record made love in a garden."

"Nonsense, darling! Eden was a quite fascinating jungle,
in which all the wild animals conversed with intelligence
and affability. You don't suppose Eve would have stood
there alone, calmly listening while the serpent talked
theology, unless conversations with animals had been an
everyday occurrence. Think how you'd flee to me, if an old
cow in the park suddenly asked you a question. But do
let's keep to the point. I've got a new plot, and I must have
a new setting."

"Why not be content to do as you have done before,
Ronnie; go on writing, simply and sincerely, of the life you
live and know?"

"Because, my dear girl, in common with the Athenians, people are always wanting either to tell or to hear some new thing. I've got hold of a jolly new thing, and I'm going to run it for all it's worth."

Helen considered this in silence.

Ronald walked over to the window, and beat a tattoo upon the *In hoc vince* pane.

"Do you see?" he asked.

"Yes," she answered, slowly. "I see your point, but I also see danger ahead. I am so anxious that, in your work, you should keep the object and motive at the highest; not putting success or popularity in their wrong place. Let success be the result of good work well done—conscientiously done. Let popularity follow unsought, simply from the fact that you have been true to yourself, and to your instinctive inspiration; that you have seen life at its best, and tried to portray it at its highest. To go rushing off to Central Africa in order to find a startling setting, is an angling after originality, which will by no means ensure doing really better work. Oh, Ronnie, my advice is: be content to stay at home, and to write truly and sincerely of the things you know."

Ronald came back to his chair; sat down, his elbows on his knees, his chin in his hands, and looked earnestly into the troubled eyes of his wife.

"But, Helen," he said, "that really is not the point. Can't you see that I am completely possessed by this new plot? Also, that Central Africa is its only possible setting? It is merely a satisfactory side-issue, that it varies my *mise en scène*."

"Must you go off there, Ronnie, in order to write it? Why not get all the newest and best books on African travel, and read up facts——"

"Never!" cried Ronald, on his feet again, and walking up and down the room. "I must be steeped in the wonderful African atmosphere, before I can sub-consciously work it into my book. No account of other men's travels could do this for me. Besides, one might get all the main things correct, yet make a slip in some little unimportant detail. Then, by and by, some Johnny would come along, who could no more have written a page of your book than he could fly, but who happens to be intimately acquainted with the locality. He ignores the plot, the character-study, all the careful work on the essentials; but he spots your trivial error concerning some completely unimportant detail. So off he writes to the papers, triumphantly airing his little tit-bit of superior information; other mediocre people take it up—and you never hear the end of it."

Helen laughed, tender amusement in her eyes.

"Ronnie dear, I admit that not many Johnnies could write your books. But most Johnnies can fly, nowadays! You must be more up to date in your similes, old boy; or you will have your wife writing to the papers, remarking that you are behind the times! But, seriously, Ronnie, you should be grateful to anybody who takes the trouble to point out an error, however small, in one of your books. You are keen that your work should be perfect; and if a mistake is mentioned, it can be set right. Why, surely you remember, when you read me the scene in the manuscript you wrote just after our marriage, in which a good lady could not sit down upon a small chair, owing to her *toupet*, I—your admiring and awestruck wife—ventured to point out that a *toupet* was not a crinoline; and you were quite grateful, Ronnie. You did not consider me an unappreciative Johnny, nor even a mediocre person! Who has, unknown to me, been trampling on your susceptibilities?"

"Nobody, thank goodness! I have never written a scene yet, of which I had not carefully verified every detail of the setting. But it has happened lots of times to people I know. Unimportant slips never seem to me to matter in another fellow's work, but they would matter desperately, horribly, appallingly in one's own. Therefore, nothing will ever induce me to place the plot of a novel of mine, in surroundings with which I am not completely familiar. Helen—I must go to Central Africa."

CHAPTER II

THE SOB OF THE WOMAN

HELEN TOOK off her riding-hat, and passed her fingers through the abundant waves of her hair.

"How long would it take you, Ronnie?"

"Well—including the journey out, and the journey back, I ought to have a clear seven months. If we could get off in a fortnight, we might be back early in November; anyway, in plenty of time for Christmas."

"Why do you say 'we,' darling?"

"Why not say 'we'? We always do, don't we?"

"Yes, dear. For three happy years it has always been 'we,' in everything. We have not been parted for longer than twelve hours at a time, Ronnie. But I fear Central Africa cannot be 'we.' I do not feel that I could go out there with you."

"Helen! Why not? I thought you would be keen on it. I thought you were game to go anywhere!" Amazement and dismay were in his eyes.

She rose slowly, went over to the mantelpiece, moved some little porcelain figures, then put them back again.

When at length she spoke, she steadied her voice with an effort.

"Ronnie dear, Central Africa is not a place for a woman."

"But, my dearest girl, a woman arrives there in my story! She crawls into the long grass with the man she loves, and disappears. Our missionary's bride did it. Where a woman could not go, *I* must not go for my local colour. Oh, I say, Helen! You won't fail me?"

He walked over to the window, and drummed again, with restless, nervous fingers, upon the *In hoc vince* pane.

She came behind him, laying her hand on his shoulder.

"Darling, it will break my heart if you think I am failing you. But, while you have been talking, I have faced the matter out, and—I must tell you at once—I cannot feel it either right or possible to go. I could not be away just now, for seven months. This place must be looked after. Think of the little church we are building in the village; the farms changing tenants this summer; the hundred and one things I, and I only, must settle and arrange. You never see the bailiff; you hardly know the tenants; you do not oversee the workpeople. So you can scarcely judge, dear Ronnie, how important is my presence here; how almost impossible it would be for me suddenly to go completely out of reach. My darling—if you keep to it, if you really intend to go, we must face the fact that it will mean, for us, a long parting."

The tension of suspense held the stillness of the room.

Then: "It is my profession," said Ronald West, huskily. "It is my career."

She moved round and faced him. They stood looking at one another, dumbly.

She knew all that was in his mind, and most that was in his heart.

He knew nothing of that which filled her mind at the moment, and only partly realised the great, unselfish love for him which filled her heart.

He was completely understood. He rested in that fact, without in the least comprehending his own lack of comprehension.

Moving close to him, she laid both hands upon his shoulders, hiding her face in silence against his breast.

He stroked her soft hair—helplessly, tenderly.

With his whole heart he loved her, leaned upon her, needed her. She had done everything for him; been everything to him.

But he meant to carry his point. He intended to go to Central Africa, and it was no sort of good pretending he did not. You never pretended with Helen, because she was through you immediately, and usually told you so.

He had not spent a single night away from her since that wonderful day when, calm and radiant, she had moved up the church in presence of an admiring crowd, and taken her place at his side.

He was practically unknown then, as a writer. No one but Helen believed in him, or understood what he had it in him to accomplish. Whereas Helen herself was the last representative of an ancient County family, owner of Hollymead Grange, and of a considerable income; courted, admired, sought after. Yet she gave herself to him, in humble tenderness. Helen had a royal way of giving. The very way she throned you in her heart, dropped you on one knee before her footstool.

He had fully justified her belief in him; but he well knew how much of his success he owed to her. Their love had taught him lessons, given him ideals which had not been his before.

But there was nothing selfish or sentimental about Helen. When the most sacred of their experiences crept into his work, and stood revealed for all the world to read; when his art transferred to hard type, and to the black and white of print and paper, the magic thrill of Helen's tenderness, so that all her friends could buy it for four shillings and sixpence, and discuss it at leisure, Helen never winced. She only smiled and said: "The world has a right to every beautiful thing we can give it. I have always felt indignant with the people who collect musical instruments which they have no intention of playing; who lock up Strads and Cremonas in glass cases, thus holding them dumb for ever to the eager ear of a listening world."

Only once, when he had put into a story a tender little name by which Helen sometimes called him, unable to resist giving his hero the bliss he, on those rare occasions, himself felt—he found a firm pencil line drawn through the words, when he looked at the proof sheets, after Helen had returned them to his desk. She never mentioned the matter to him, nor did he speak of it to her; but his hero had to forgo that particular thrill, and it was a long time before Ronald himself heard again the words Helen had deleted.

He heard them now, however—murmured very softly; and he caught her to him with sudden passion, kissing her hair.

Yet he meant to go. *In hoc vince.* He must conquer his very need of her, if it came between him and the best thing he had yet done in his work.

He could not face the thought of the parting; but there was no need to face that as yet. A whole fortnight intervened. It is useless to suffer a pang until the pang is actually upon you. Besides, every experience—however hard to bear—is of value. How much more harrowing and vivid would be his next description of a parting——

Then, suddenly, Ronald felt ashamed. His arms dropped from around her. He knew himself unworthy—in a momentary flash of self-revelation he knew himself utterly unworthy—of Helen's generous love, and noble womanhood.

"My wife," he said, "I won't go. It isn't worth it."

Her arms strained around him, and he heard her sob; and alas—it was the sob of the woman in the long grass, when she clung to the man who had crawled out first. His plot stood out to him once more as the supreme thing.

"At least," he added, "it wouldn't be worth it, if it costs

you so much. It *is* my strongest plot, but I will give it up if you would rather I stayed at home."

Then Helen loosed her detaining arms, and lifting a brave white face, smiled at him through her tears.

"No, Ronnie," she said. "I promised when we married, always to help you with your work and to make it easy. I am not going to fail you now. If the new book requires a parting, we will face it bravely. At the present moment we both need luncheon, and I must get out of my habit. Ring, and tell them we shall not be ready for a quarter of an hour, there's a dear boy! And think of something really funny to tell me at lunch. Afterwards we will discuss plans."

She had reached the door when Ronald suddenly called after her: "Helen! Hadn't you something to tell me, too?"

She turned in the doorway. Her face was gay with smiles.

"Oh, mine must wait," she said. "Your new plot, and the wonderful journey it involves, require our undivided attention."

The sun shone very brightly just then. It touched the halo of Helen's soft hair, turning it to gold. *In hoc vince* gleamed upon the pane.

For a moment she stood in the doorway, giving him a chance to insist upon hearing that which she had to tell. But Ronald, easily satisfied, turned and rang the bell.

"All right, sweet," he said. "How lovely you look in the sunshine! If it was business, or anything worrying, I would certainly rather not hear it now. You have bucked me up splendidly, Helen. Seven months seem nothing; and my whole mind is bounding forward into my story. I really must give you an outline of the plot." He followed her into the hall. "Helen! Do come back for a minute."

But Helen was half-way up the stairs. He heard her laugh as she reached the landing.

"I am hungry, dear," she called over the banisters, "and so are you, only you don't know it! Crawl out of your long grass, and make yourself presentable before the gong sounds; or I shall send bananas for one, to your study!"

"All right!" he shouted; gave Helen's message to the butler; then went through the billiard-room, whistling gaily.

"Why, she is as keen as I am," he said to himself, as he turned on the hot and cold water taps. "And she is perfectly right about not coming with me. Of course it's jolly hard to leave her; but I believe I shall do better work alone."

His mind went back to Helen's bright face in the doorway. He realised her mastery, for his sake, of her own dread of the parting.

"What a brick she is!" he said. "Always so perfectly plucky. I don't believe any other fellow in the world has such a wife as Helen!"

CHAPTER III

HELEN TAKES THE INITIATIVE

HAVING ONCE made up her mind that it was right and wise to let Ronnie go, Helen did not falter. She immediately took control of all necessary arrangements. Nothing was forgotten. Ronnie's outfit was managed with as little trouble to himself as possible. They dealt together, in a gay morning at the Stores, with all interesting items, but those he called "the dull things" apparently selected themselves. Anyway, they all appeared in his room, when the time came for packing.

So whole-hearted was his wife's interest in the undertaking, that Ronnie almost began to look upon it as her plan.

It was she who arranged routes and booked his passages. When Cook's cheque had to be written, it was a large one.

Helen took out her cheque book.

"No, no, dear," said Ronnie. "I must pay it out of my own earnings. It is a literary speculation."

Helen hesitated. She knew Ronnie did not realise how much the new building and necessary repairs on the estate were costing her this year.

"What is your balance at the bank, Ronnie?"

"I haven't the remotest idea."

"Darling, why don't you make a note of your last balance on your counterfoil? Then at any moment you can add up all subsequent cheques and see at a glance how you stand."

"Yes, I know, you have explained all that to me before, Helen. But, you see, most of my counterfoils are blank! I forget to fill them in. You can't write books, and also keep accounts. If you really think it important, I might give up the former, and turn my whole attention to the latter."

"Don't be silly, dear! You are blessed with a wife who keeps a careful account of every penny of her own. But I know nothing of your earnings and spendings, excepting when you suddenly remark at breakfast: 'Hullo! Here's a useful little cheque for a thousand'—in much the same tone of voice as you exclaim the next minute: 'Hullo! What excellent hot-buttered toast!' Ronnie, I wish you would manage to invest rather more."

"My dear girl, I have invested heaps! You made me. But what is the use of saving money when there are only ourselves to consider? We may as well spend it, and have a good time. If there were kiddies to leave it to, it would be different. I had so long of being impecunious, that I particularly enjoy feeling bottomless! Besides, each year will bring in more. This African book ought to be worth all the rest put together."

Helen was silent; but she sighed as she filled in Cook's cheque and signed it. Ronald had spoken so lightly of the great disappointment of their married life. It was always difficult to get Ronnie to take things seriously. The fact was: he took *himself* so seriously, that he was obliged to compensate by taking everything and everybody else rather lightly. No doubt this arrangement of relative values, made for success. Ronnie's success had been very rapid, and very brilliant. He accepted it with the unconscious modesty of the true artist; his work meaning immeasurably more to him than that which his work brought him, either in praise or pennies.

But Helen gloried in the praise, kept a watchful eye, so far as he would let her, on the pennies; and herself ministered to the idea that all else must be subservient, where Ronnie's literary career was concerned.

She was ministering to it now, at a personal cost known only to her own brave heart.

CHAPTER IV

FIRELIGHT IN THE STUDIO

IT WAS Ronnie's last evening in England. The parting, which had seemed so far away, must take place on the morrow. It took all Helen's bright courage to keep up Ronnie's spirits.

After dinner they sat together in a room they still called the studio, although Helen had given up her painting, soon after their marriage.

It was a large old-fashioned room, oak-panelled and spacious.

A huge mirror, in a massive gilt frame, hung upon the wall opposite door and fireplace, reaching from the ceiling to the parquet floor.

Ronald, who used the studio as a smoking-room, had

introduced three or four deep wicker chairs, comfortably cushioned, and a couple of Oriental tables.

The fireplace lent itself grandly in winter to great log-fires, when the crimson curtains were drawn in ample folds over the many windows, shutting out the dank bleakness of the park without, and imparting a look of cosiness to the empty room.

A dozen old family portraits—banished from more important places, because their expressions annoyed Ronnie —were crowded into whatever space was available, and glowered down, from the bad light to which they had been relegated, on the very modern young man whose uncomplimentary remarks had effected their banishment, and who sprawled luxuriously in the firelight, monarch of all he surveyed, in the domain which for centuries had been their own.

The only other thing in the room was a piano, on which Ronnie very effectively and very inaccurately strummed by ear; and on which Helen, with careful skill, played his accompaniments, when he was seized with a sudden desire to sing.

Ronald's music was always a perplexity to Helen. There was a quality about it so extraordinarily, so unusually, beautiful; combined with an entire lack of method or of training, and a quite startling ignorance of the most rudimentary rules.

On one occasion, during a sharp attack of influenza, when he had insisted upon being down and about, with a temperature of 104, he suddenly rose from the depths of a chair in which he had been lying, talking wild and feverish nonsense; stumbled over to the piano, dropped heavily upon the stool, then proceeded to play and sing, in a way which brought tears to his wife's eyes, while her heart stood still with anxiety and wonder.

Yet, when she mentioned it a few days later, he appeared

to have forgotten all about it, turning the subject with
almost petulant abruptness.

But, on this their last evening together, the piano stood
unheeded. They seemed only to want two chairs, and each
other.

She could hardly take her eyes from his face, remembering
how many months must pass, before she could see him
again. Yet it was Ronnie who made moan, and Helen who
bravely comforted; turning as often as possible to earnest
discussion of his plot and its possibilities. But after a while
even she went under, to the thought of the nearness of the
parting.

Though it was late in April, the evenings were chilly; a
fire glowed in the grate.

Presently Ronnie rose, turned off the electric light, and
seated himself on the rug in the firelight, resting his head
against his wife's knees.

Silently she passed her fingers through his hair.

Something in the quality of her silence turned Ronald's
thoughts from himself to her alone. "Helen," he said, "I
hate to be leaving you. Shall you be very lonely?"

She could not answer.

"You are sure your good old Mademoiselle Victorine is
coming to be with you?"

"Yes, dear. She holds herself in readiness to come as
soon as I feel able to send for her. She and I lived alone
together here during eighteen months, after Papa's death.
We were very quietly happy. I do not see why we should
not be happy again."

"What shall you do all day?"

"Well, I shall have my duties in the village and on the
estate; and, for our recreation, we shall read French and
German, and do plenty of music. Mademoiselle Victorine
delights in playing what she calles 'des à quatre mains,' which

consist in our both prancing vigorously upon the same piano; she, steadily punishing the bass; while I fly after her, on the more lively treble. It is good practice; it has its fascinations, and it will take the place of riding, for me."

"Shan't you ride, Helen?"

"No, Ronnie; not without you."

"Will you and Mademoiselle Victorine drive your four-in-hands in here?"

"No, not in here, darling. I don't think I shall be able to bear to touch the piano on which you play to me."

"I don't play," said Ronnie. "I strum."

"True, dear. You often strum. But sometimes you play quite wonderfully. I wish you had been properly taught!"

"I always hated being taught anything," said Ronald. "I like doing things, without learning to do them. And I know what you mean, about the times when I really play. But, excepting when the mood is on me, I don't care to think of those times. I never feel really myself when it happens. I seem to be listening to somebody else playing, and trying to remember something I have hopelessly forgotten. It gives me a strained, uncanny feeling, Helen."

"Does it, darling? Then let us talk of something else. Oh, Ronnie, you must promise me to take care of your health out in that climate? I believe you are going at the very worst time of year."

"I have to know it at its worst and at its hottest," he said. "But I shall be all right. I'm strong as a horse, and sound in wind and limb."

"I hope you will get good food."

He laughed. "I expect to have to live on just whatever I can shoot or grub up. You see, the more completely I leave all civilisation, the more correctly I shall get my 'copy.' I can't crawl into the long grass, carrying tins of sardines and bottles of Bass!"

"You might take meat lozenges," suggested Ronnie's wife.

"Meat lozenges, darling, are concentrated nastiness. I felt like an unhealthy bullock the whole of the rest of the day when, to please you, I sucked one while we were mountain climbing. I propose living on interesting and unique fruits and roots—all the things which correspond to locusts and wild honey. But, Helen, I am afraid there will be quite a long time during which I shall not be able either to send or to receive letters. We shall have to console ourselves with the trite old saying: 'No news is good news.' Of course, so far as I am concerned, it would be useless to hear of any cause for anxiety or worry, when I could not possibly get back, or deal with it."

"You shall not hear of any worries, or have any anxieties, darling. If difficulties arise, I will deal with them. You must keep a perfectly free mind, all the time. For my part, I will try not to give way to panics about you, if you will promise to cable occasionally, and to write as often as you can."

"*You* won't go and get ill, will you, Helen?"

She smiled, laying her cheek on the top of his head, as she bent over him.

"I never get ill, darling. Like you, I am sound in wind and limb. We are a most healthy couple."

"We shall both be thirty, Helen, before we meet again. You will attain to that advanced age a month before I shall. On your birthday I shall drink your health in some weird concoction of juices; and I shall say to all the lions and tigers, hippopotamuses, cockatrices and asps, sitting round my camp fire: 'You will hardly believe it, my heathen hearers, out in this well-ordered jungle, where the female is kept in her proper place—but my wife has had the cheek to march up to-day into the next decade, leaving me behind in the youthful twenties!'—Oh, Helen, I wish we had a little kiddie playing around! I am tired of being the youngest of the family."

She clasped both hands about his throat. He might have heard the beating of her heart—had he been listening.

"Ronald, that is a joy which may yet be ours—some day. But my writer of romances, who is such a stickler for grammatical accuracy, is surely the *younger* of a family of *two*!"

"Oh, grammar be——relegated to the library!" cried Ronnie, laughing. "And you really presume too much on that one short month, Helen. You often treat me as if I were an infant."

The smile in her eyes held the mother look, in its yearning tenderness.

"Ronnie dear, you *are* so very much younger than I, in many ways; and you always will be. Unlike the 'Infant of Days,' if you live to be a hundred years old, you will still die young; a child in heart, full of youth's joyous joy of living. You must not mind if your wife occasionally treats you as though you were a dear big baby, requiring maternal care and petting. You are such a veritable boy sometimes, and it soothes the yearning for a little son of yours to cuddle in her arms, when she plays that her big boy is something of a baby."

Ronald took her left hand from about his neck, and kissed it tenderly.

This was his only answer, but his silence meant more to Helen than speech. Words flowed so readily to express his surface thoughts; but when words suddenly and unexpectedly failed, a deeper depth had been reached; and in that silence, his wife found comfort and content.

Ronnie was not all ripples. There was more beneath than the shifting shallows. Deep, still pools were there, and rocks on which might eventually be built a beacon-light for the souls of men. But, as yet, it took Helen's clear and faithful eyes to discern the pools; to perceive the possible strong foundations.

"Do you remember," he said presently, "the Dalmains coming over last January, with their little Geoff? When I saw that jolly little chap trotting about, and looking up at his mother with big shining eyes, full of trustful love and innocent courage, absolutely unafraid—notwithstanding her rather peremptory manner, and apparently stern discipline—I felt that it must be the making of two people to have such a little son as that, depending upon them to show him how to grow up right. One would simply be obliged to live up to his baby belief in one; wouldn't one Helen?"

"Yes, darling; we—we should."

"I hope you will see a lot of the Dalmains while I am away. Try to put in a good long visit there. And she would come over, if you wanted her, wouldn't she?"

"Yes; she will come if I want her."

"You and she are great friends," pursued Ronnie, "aren't you? I find her alarming. When she looks at me, I feel such a worm. I want to slide into a hole and hide. But there is never a hole to be found. I have to remain erect, handing tea and bread-and-butter, while I mentally grovel. I almost pray that a hungry blackbird or a prying thrush may chance to come my way, and consider me juicy and appetising. You remember—the Vicar and *Mrs.* Vicar came to tea that day. She wore brown spots. But even the priestly blackbird, and the Levitical thrush, passed me by on the other side."

"Oh, Ronnie, how silly! I know Jane admires your books, darling!"

"She considers me quite unfit to tie your shoe-strings."

"Ronnie, be quiet! You would not be afraid of her, had you ever known what it was to turn to her in trouble or difficulty. She helped me through an awfully bad time six months before I met you. She showed me the right thing to do, then stood by me while I did it. There is nobody in the whole world quite like her."

"Well, send for her if you get into any troubles while I am away. I shall feel quite brave about her being here, when I am safely hidden in the long grass!"

"Is there any possible chance that you will get back sooner than you think, Ronnie?"

"Hardly. Not before November, anyway. And yesterday my publishers were keen that I should put in a night at Leipzig on my way home, and a night at The Hague; show whatever 'copy' I have to firms there, and make arrangements for German and Dutch translations to appear as soon as possible after the English edition is out. I think I may as well do this, and return by the Hook of Holland. I enjoy the night-crossing, and like reaching London early in the morning. By the way, haven't you a cousin of some sort living at Leipzig?"

"Yes; my first cousin, Aubrey Treherne. He is studying music, and working on compositions of his own, I believe. He lives in a flat in the Grassi Strasse."

"All right. Put his address in my pocket book. I will look him up. My special chum, Dick Cameron, is to be out there in November, investigating one of their queer water-cures. I wish you knew Dick Cameron, Helen. I shall hope to see him, too. Has your cousin a spare room in his flat?"

"I do not know. Ronnie, Aubrey Treherne is not a good man. He is not a man you should trust."

"Darling, you don't necessarily trust a fellow because he puts you up for the night. But I dare say Dick will find me a room."

"Aubrey is not a good man," repeated Helen, firmly.

"Dear, we are none of us good."

"*You* are, Ronnie—in the sense I mean, or I should not have married you."

"Oh, then, yes *please*!" said Ronnie. "I am very, very good!"

He laughed up at her, but Helen's face was grave. Then a sudden thought brightened it.

"If you really go to Leipzig, Ronnie, could you look in at Zimmermann's—a first-rate place for musical instruments of all kinds—and choose me a small organ for the new church? I saw a little beauty the other day at Huntingford; a perfect tone, twelve stops, and quite easy to play. They had had it sent over from Leipzig. It cost only twenty-four pounds. In England, one could hardly have bought so good an instrument for less than forty. If you could choose one with a really sweet tone, and have it shipped over here, I should be grateful."

"With pleasure, darling. I enjoy trying all sorts of instruments. But why economise over the organ? If my wife fancied a hundred guinea organ, I could give it her."

"No, you couldn't, Ronnie. You must not be extravagant."

"I am not extravagant, dear. Buying things one can afford is not extravagance."

"Sometimes it is. Extravagance is not spending money. But it is paying a higher price for a thing than the actual need demands, or than the circumstances justify. I considered you extravagant last winter when you paid five guineas for a box at Olympia, intended to hold eight people, and sat in it, in solitary grandeur, alone with your wife."

"I know you did," said Ronnie. "You left me no possible loophole for doubt in the matter. But your quite mistaken view, on that occasion, arose from an incorrect estimate of values. I paid one pound, six shillings and threepence for the two seats, and three pounds, eighteen and ninepence for the pleasure of sitting alone with my wife, and thought it cheap at that. It was a far lower price than the actual need demanded; therefore, by your own showing, it was not extravagant."

"Oh, what a boy it is!" sighed Helen, with a little gesture

of despair. "Then, last Christmas, Ronnie, you insisted upon fêting the old people with all kinds of unnecessary luxuries. They had always been quite content with wholesome bread-and-butter, plum cake, and nice hot tea. They did not require *pâté de foie gras* and champagne, nor did they understand or really enjoy them. One old lady, in considerable distress, confided to me the fact that the champagne tasted to her 'like physic with a fizzle in it.' It made most of them ill, Ronnie, and cost at least eight times as much as my simple Christmas parties of other years. So don't go and spend an unnecessary sum on an elaborate, and probably less useful, instrument. I will write you full particulars when the time comes. Oh, Ronnie, you will be so nearly home, by then! How shall I wait?"

"I shall love to feel I have something to do for you in Leipzig," said Ronnie; "and I enjoy poking about among crowds of queer instruments. I should like to have played in Nebuchadnezzar's band. I should have played the sackbut, because I haven't the faintest notion how you work the thing—whether you blow into it, or pull it in and out, or tread upon it; nor what manner of surprising sound it emits, when you do any or all of these things. I love springing surprises on myself and on other people; and I know I do best the things which, if I considered the matter beforehand, I shouldn't have the veriest ghost of a notion how to set about doing. That, darling, is inspiration! I should have played the sackbut by inspiration; whereupon Nebuchadnezzar would instantly have had me cast into the burning fiery furnace."

"Oh, Ronnie, I wish I could laugh! But to-morrow is so near. What shall I do when there is nobody here to tell me silly stories?"

"Ask Mademoiselle Victorine to try her hand at it. Say: 'Chère mademoiselle, s'il-vous-plaît, racontez-moi une extrêmement sotte histoire'."

"Ronnie, do stop chaffing! Go and play me something really beautiful, and sing very softly, as you did the other night; so that I can hear the tones of the piano and your voice vibrating together."

"No," said Ronnie, "I can't. I have a cast-iron lump in my throat just now, and not a note could pass it. Besides, I don't really play the piano."

He stretched out his foot, and kicked a log into the fire.

The flame shot up, illumining the room. The log-fire, and the two seated near it, were reflected fitfully in the distant mirror.

"Helen, there is one instrument, above all others, which I have always longed to play; yet I have never even held one in my hand."

"What instrument is that, darling?"

"The violoncello," said Ronnie, sitting up and turning towards her as he spoke. "When I think of a 'cello I seem as if I knew exactly how it would feel to hold it between my knees, press my fingers up and down the yielding strings, and draw the bow across them. Helen—if I had a 'cello here to-night, you would listen to sounds of such exquisite throbbing beauty, that you would forget everything in this world, my wife, excepting that I love you."

His eyes shone in the firelight. An older look of deeper strength and of fuller manly vigour came into his face. The glow of love transfigured it.

With an uncontrollable sob, Helen stooped and laid her lips on his.

The clock struck midnight.

"Oh, Ronnie," she said; "oh, Ronnie! It is _to-day_, now! No longer to-morrow—but to-day!"

He sprang to his feet, took her hand, and drew her to the door.

"Come, Helen," he said.

PART II

CHAPTER V

THE INFANT OF PRAGUE

TWO MEN, in a flat at Leipzig, sat on either side of a tall porcelain stove.

The small door in the stove stood open, letting a ruddy glow shine from within, a poor substitute for the open fires blazing merrily in England on this chill November evening; yet giving visible evidence of the heat contained within those cool-looking blue and white embossed tiles.

The room itself was a curious mixture of the taste of the Leipzig landlady, who owned and had furnished it, and of the Englishman studying music, who was its temporary tenant.

The high-backed sofa, upholstered in red velvet, stood stiffly against the wall, awaiting the 'guest of honour,' who never arrived. It served, however, as a resting-place for a violin, and a pile of music; while, on the opposite side of the room, partly eclipsing a fancy picture of Goethe, stood a chamber organ, open, and displaying a long row of varied stops.

Books and music were piled upon every available flat space, saving the table; upon which lay the remains of supper.

Of the three easy chairs placed in a semicircle near the stove, two were occupied; but against the empty chair in the centre, its dark brown polished surface reflecting the glow of the fire, leaned a beautiful old violoncello. The metal point of its foot made a slight dent in the parquet floor.

The younger of the two men sat well forward, elbows on knees, eyes alight with excitement, intently gazing at the 'cello.

The other lay back in his chair, his thin sensitive fingers carefully placed tip to tip, his deep-set eyes scrutinising his companion. When he spoke his voice was calm and deliberate, his manner exceedingly quiet. His method of conversation was of the kind which drew out the full confidence of others, while at the same time carefully insinuating, rather than frankly expressing, ideas of his own.

"What a rum fellow you must be, West, to pay a hundred and fifty pounds for an instrument you have no notion of playing. Is it destined to be kept under lock and key in a glass case?"

"Certainly not," said Ronald West. "I shall be able to play it when I try; and I shall try, as soon as I get home."

"Give us a sample here."

"No, not here. I particularly wish to play it first with Helen, in the room where I told her a 'cello was the instrument I had always wanted. Oh, I say, isn't it a beauty! Look at those curves, and that wonderful polish, like the richest brown of the very darkest horse-chestnut you ever saw in a bursting burl See how the silver strings shine in the firelight, against the black ebony of the finger-board! It was made at Prague, and it is a hundred and fifty years old. I call it the Infant of Prague."

"Why the 'Infant'?"

"Because you have to be so careful not to bump its head as you carry it about. Also isn't there a verse somewhere, about an Infant of Days who was a hundred years old, and young at that? Helen will love the Infant. She will polish it with a silk handkerchief, and make a bed for it on the sofa! I shan't write to her about it. I shall bring it home as a surprise."

He took his eyes from the 'cello and looked across at Helen's cousin; but Aubrey Treherne instantly shifted his gaze to the unconscious Infant.

"Tell me how you came across it. There is no doubt you

have been fortunate enough to pick up an instrument of extraordinary value and beauty."

"Ah, you realise that?" cried Ronald. "Good! Well, you shall hear exactly what happened. I arrived here early this morning, put up at a hotel, and sallied out to interview the publishers. I had a mass of 'copy' to show them, because I have been writing incessantly the whole way home. Curiously enough, since I left Africa, I have scarcely needed any sleep. Snatches of half an hour seem all I require. It is convenient when one has a vast amount of work to get through in a short space of time."

"Very convenient. Just the reverse of the sleeping sickness."

"Rather! I was never fitter in my life—as I told Dick Cameron."

Aubrey Treherne glanced at the bright burning eyes and flushed face—the feverish blood showing, even through the tan of Africa.

"Yes, you look jolly fit," he said. "Who is Dick Cameron?"

"A great chum of mine. We met, as boys in Edinburgh, and were at school together. He is the son of Colonel Cameron, of Transvaal fame, killed while leading a charge. Dick has done awfully well in the medical, passed all necessary exams, and taken every possible degree. He is now looking out for a practice, and meanwhile a big man in London has sent him out to investigate, one of these queer water friction cures—professes to cure cataract and cancer and every known disease, by simply sitting you in a tub, and rubbing you down with a dish-cloth. Dick Cameron says—Hullo! Why are we talking of Dick Cameron? I thought I was telling you about the 'cello."

"You are telling me about the 'cello," said Aubrey, quietly. "But in order to arrive at the 'cello we had to hear about your visit to the publishers with your mass of manuscript, which resulted from having acquired in Central Africa the useful habit of not needing more than half an hour of sleep in the twenty-four; which, possibly, Dick Cameron did not consider sufficient. Doctors are apt to be faddy in such matters. Whereupon you, naturally, told him you were perfectly fit."

"Ah, yes, I remember," said Ronnie. "Am I spinning rather a yarn?"

"Not at all, my dear fellow. Do not hurry. We have the whole evening before us—night, if necessary. You can put in your half-hour at any time, I suppose; and I can dispense with sleep for once. It is not often one has the chance of spending a night in the company of a noted author, an African traveller straight from the jungle, and the man who has married one's favourite cousin. I am all delighted attention. What did your friend Dick Cameron say?"

"Well, I met him as I was hurrying back to the hotel, carrying the Infant, which did not appear to advantage in the exceedingly plain brown canvas bag, which was all they could give me at Zimmermann's. When I get home I shall consult Helen, and we shall order the best case procurable."

"Naturally. Probably Helen will advise a bassinet by night, and a perambulator by day."

Ronnie looked perplexed. "Why a bassinet?" he said.

"The *Infant*, you know."

"Oh—ah, yes, I see. Well, of course I wanted to introduce the Infant properly to Dick Cameron, but he objected when I began taking it out of its bag in the street. He suggested that it might take cold—it certainly is a dank day. Also that there are so many by-laws and regulations in Leipzig connected with things you may not do in the streets, that probably if you took a 'cello out of its case and stood admiring it in the midst of the crowded thoroughfare, you would get run in by a policeman. Dick said: 'Arrest of the Infant of Prague in the streets of Leipzig' would make just the kind of sensational headline beloved by newspapers. I realised that he was right. It would have distressed Helen, besides being a most unfortunate way for her to hear first of the Infant. Helen is a great stickler for respectability."

Aubrey Treherne's pale countenance turned a shade paler. His thin lips curved into the semblance of a smile.

"Ah, yes," he said, "of course. Helen is a great stickler for respectability. Well? So you gave up undressing your Infant in the street?"

Again Ronnie's eager face took on a look of perplexity.

"I did not propose undressing it," he said. "I only wanted to take it out of its bag."

"I see. Quite a simple matter. Well? Owing to our absurd police regulations you were prevented from doing this. What happened next?"

"Dick suggested that we should go to his rooms. Arrived there he ceased to take any interest in my 'cello, clapped me into a chair, and stuck a beastly thermometer into my mouth."

"Doctors are such enthusiasts," murmured Aubrey Treherne. "They can never let their own particular trade alone. I suppose he also felt your pulse and looked at your tongue."

"Rather! Then he said I had no business to be walking about with a temperature of 103. I was so much annoyed that I promptly smashed the thermometer, and we had a fine chase after the quicksilver. You never saw anything like it! It ran like a rabbit, in and out of the nooks and corners of the chair, until at last it disappeared through a crack in the floor; went to ground, you know. Doesn't Helen look well on horseback?"

"Charming. I suppose you easily convinced your friend that his diagnosis was rubbish?"

"Of course I did. I told him I had never felt better in

my life. But I drank the stuff he gave me, simply to save further bother; also another dose which he brought to the hotel. Then he insisted on leaving a bottle out of which I am to take a dose every three hours on the journey home. I did not know old Dick was such a crank."

"Probably it is the result of sitting in a tub and being scrubbed with a dish-cloth. Did he know you were coming here?"

"Yes; he picked up my pocket-book, found your address, and made a note of it. He said he should probably look us up at about ten o'clock this evening. I told him I might be here pretty late. I did not know you were going to be so kind as to fetch my things from the hotel and put me up. You really are most——"

"Delighted, my dear fellow. Honoured!" said Aubrey Treherne. "Now tell me about the finding of the 'cello."

"I interviewed the publishers, and I hope it is all right. But they seemed rather hurried and vague, and anxious to get me off the premises. No doubt I shall fare better in courteous little Holland. Then I went on to Zimmermann's to choose Helen's organ. I found exactly what she wanted, and at the price she wished. On my way downstairs I found myself in a large room full of violoncellos—dozens of them. They were hanging in glass cases; they were ranged along the top. Then I suddenly felt impelled to look to the top of the highest cabinet, and there I saw the Infant! I knew instantly that that was the 'cello I *must* have. It seemed mine already. It seemed as if it always had been mine. I asked to be shown some violoncellos. They produced two or three, in which I took no interest. Then I said: 'Get down that dark brown one, third from the end.' They lifted it down, and, from the moment I touched it, I knew it must be mine! They told me it was made at Prague, a hundred and fifty years ago, and its price was three thousand marks. Luckily, I had my cheque-book in my pocket, also my card, Helen's card, my publisher's letter of introduction to the firm here, and my own letter of credit from my bankers. So they expressed themselves willing to take my cheque. I wrote it then and there, and marched out with the Infant. I first called it the Infant on the stairs, as we were leaving Zimmermann's, because I almost bumped its head! Isn't it a beauty?"

"Undoubtedly it is."

"They put on a new set of the very best strings," continued Ronnie; "supplied me with a good bow, and threw in a cake of rosin."

"What did you pay for the organ?" inquired Aubrey Treherne.

"Twenty-four pounds. Helen would not have a more expensive one. She is always telling me not to be extravagant."

"That, my dear boy, invariably happens to an impecunious fellow who marries a rich wife."

Ronnie flushed. "I am impecunious no longer," he said, "During the past twelve months I have made, by my books. a larger income than my wife's."

"I can well believe it," said Aubrey, cordially. "But I suppose she can never forget the fact that, when you married her, she paid your debts."

Ronald West sprang to his feet.

"Confound you!" he said violently. "What do you mean? Helen never paid my debts! She found them out, I admit; but I paid them every one myself, with the first cheque I received from my publishers. I demand an explanation of your statement."

The other two members of the trio round the stove appeared completely unmoved by the fury of the young man who had leapt to his feet. The Infant of Prague leaned calmly against its chair, reflecting the fire in its polished surface, and pressing its one sharp foot into the parquet.

Aubrey smiled, deprecatingly, and waved Ronnie back to his seat.

"My dear fellow, I am sure I beg your pardon. My cousin certainly gave her family to understand that she had paid your debts. No doubt this was not the case. We all know that women are somewhat given to exaggeration and inaccuracy. Think no more of it."

Ronnie sat down moodily in his chair.

"It was unlike Helen," he said, "and it was a lie. I shall find out with whom it originated. But you are a good fellow to take my word about it at once. I am obliged to you, Treherne."

"Don't mention it, West. Men rarely lie to one another. On the other hand women rarely speak the truth. What will my good cousin say to one hundred and fifty pounds being paid for a 'cello?"

"It will be no business of hers," said Ronnie, angrily. "I can do as I choose with my own earnings."

"I doubt it," smiled Aubrey Treherne. "The man who married my cousin Helen, was bound to surrender his independence and creep under her thumb. I am grateful to you for having saved me from that fate. As no doubt she has told you, she refused me shortly before she accepted you."

Ronald's start of surprise proved at once to Aubrey his complete ignorance of the whole matter.

"I had no idea you were ever in love with my wife," he said.

"Nor was I, my dear fellow," sneered Aubrey Treherne. "Others, besides yourself, were after your wife's money."

A sense of impotence seized Ronald, in nightmare grip. Indignant and furious, he yet felt absolutely unable to contradict or to explain.

Suddenly he seemed to hear Helen's voice saying earnestly: "My cousin Aubrey is not a good man, Ronnie; he is not a man you should trust."

This vivid remembrance of Helen, brought him to his senses.

"I prefer not to discuss my wife," he said, with quiet dignity; "nor my relations with her. Let us talk of something else."

"By all means, my dear fellow," replied Aubrey. "You must pardon the indiscretion of cousinly interest. Tell me of your new book. Have you settled upon a title?"

But the instinct of authorship now shielded Ronnie.

"I never talk of my books, excepting to Helen, until they are finished," he said.

"Quite right," agreed Aubrey, cordially. "But you might tell me why this one took you to Central Africa. Is it a book of travels?"

"No; it is a love-story. But the scene is laid in wild places—ah, such places! One cannot possibly understand, until one gets there and does it, what it is like to leave civilisation behind, and crawl into long grass thirteen feet high!"

"It sounds weirdly fascinating," remarked Aubrey. "So unusual a setting, must mean a remarkable plot."

"It is the strongest thing I have done yet," said Ronnie, with enthusiasm.

Aubrey smiled, surveying Ronnie's eager face with slow enjoyment. He was mentally recalling phrases from reviews he had written for various literary columns, on Ronnie's work. Already he began wording the terse sentences in which he would point out the feebleness and lack of literary merit, in "the strongest thing" Ronnie had done yet. It might be well to know something more about it.

"It will be very unlike your other books," he suggested.

"Yes," explained Ronnie, expanding. "You see they were all absolutely English; just of our own set, and our own surroundings. I wanted something new. I couldn't go on letting my hero make love in an English garden."

"If you wanted a variety," suggested Aubrey Treherne, "you might have let him make love in another man's garden. Stolen fruits are sweet! There is always a fascination about trespassing."

"No, thank you," said Ronnie. "That would be Paradise Lost."

"Or Paradise Regained," murmured Aubrey.

"I think not. Besides—Helen reads my books."

"Oh, I see," sneered Aubrey. "So your wife draws the line?"

"I don't know what you mean," replied Ronnie. "Falsehood, frailty, and infidelity, do not appeal to me as subjects for romance. But, if they did, I certainly should not feel free to put a line into one of my books which I should be ashamed to see my own wife reading."

"Oh, safe and excellent standard!" mocked Aubrey Treherne. "No wonder you go down with the British public."

"I think, if you don't mind," said Ronald, with some heat, "we will cease to discuss my books and my public."

"Then there is but one subject left to us," smiled Aubrey —"The Infant of Prague! Let us concentrate our attention upon this entirely congenial topic. I wonder how long this dear child has remained dumb. I have seen many fine instruments in my time, West, but I am inclined to think your 'cello is the finest I have yet come across. Do you mind if I tune it, and try the strings?"

Ronnie's pleasure and enthusiasm were easily rekindled.

"Do," he said. "I am grateful. I do not even know the required notes."

Aubrey, leaning forward, carefully lifted the instrument, resting it against his knees. He took a tuning-fork from his pocket.

"It is tuned in fifths," he said. "The open strings are A, D, G, C. You can remember them, because they stand for 'Allowable Delights Grow Common-place'; or, read the other way up: 'Courage Gains Desired Aims.'"

With practised skill he rapidly tightened the four strings into harmony; then, after carefully rosining the bow, rasped it with uncertain touch across them. The Infant squealed, as if in dire pain. Ronnie winced, obviously restraining himself with an effort from snatching his precious 'cello out of Aubrey's hands.

It did not strike him as peculiar that a man who played the violin with ease, should not be able to draw a clear tone from the open strings of a 'cello.

"I don't seem to make much of it," said Aubrey. "The 'cello is a difficult instrument to play, and requires long practice." And again he rasped the bow across the strings.

The Infant's wail of anguish gained in volume.

Ronnie sprang up, holding out eager hands.

"Let *me* try," he said. "It must be able to make a better sound than that!"

As he placed the 'cello between his knees, a look of rapt content came into his face. He slipped his left hand up and down the neck, letting his fingers glide gently along the strings.

Aubrey watched him narrowly.

Ronnie lifted the bow; then he paused. A sudden remembrance seemed to arrest the action in mid-air.

He laid his left hand firmly on the shoulder of the Infant, out of reach of the tempting strings.

"I am not going to play," he said. "The very first time I really play, must be in the studio, and Helen must be there. But I will just sound the open strings."

He looked down upon the 'cello and waited, the light of expectation brightening in his face.

Aubrey Treherne noted the remarkable correctness of the position he had unconsciously assumed.

Then Ronnie, raising the bow, drew it, with unfaltering touch, across the silver depths of lower C.

A rich, full note, rising, falling, vibrating, filled the room. The Infant of Prague was singing. A master-hand had waked its voice once more.

Ronnie's head swam. A hot mist was before his eyes. His breath came in short sobs. He had completely forgotten the sardonic face of his wife's cousin, in the chair opposite.

Then the hot mist cleared. He raised the bow once more, and drew it across G.

G merged into D without a pause. Then, with a strong triumphant sweep, he sounded A.

The four open strings of the 'cello had given forth their full sweetness and power.

"Helen, oh, Helen!" said Ronnie.

Then he looked up, and saw Aubrey Treherne.

He laughed, rather unsteadily. "I thought I was at home." he said. "For the moment it seemed as if I must be at home. I was experiencing the purest joy I have known since I left Helen. What do you think of my 'cello, man? Isn't it wonderful?"

"It is very wonderful," said Aubrey Treherne. "Your Infant is all you hoped. The tone is perfect. But what is still more wonderful is that you—who believe yourself never to have handled a 'cello before—can set the strings vibrating with such unerring skill; such complete mastery. Of course, to me, the mystery is no mystery. The reason of it all is perfectly clear."

"What is the reason of it all?" inquired Ronnie, eagerly.

"In a former existence, dear boy," said Aubrey Treherne, slowly, "You were a great master of the 'cello. Probably the Infant of Prague was your favourite instrument. It called to you from its high place in the 'cello room at Zimmermann's, as it has been calling to you for years; only, at last, it made you hear. It was your own, and you knew it. You would have bought it, had its price been a thousand pounds. You could not have left the place without the Infant in your possession."

Ronald's feverish flush deepened. His eyes grew more burningly bright.

"What an extraordinary idea!" he said. "I don't think Helen would like it, and I am perfectly certain Helen would not believe it. "

"You cannot refuse to believe a truth because it does not happen to appeal to your wife," said Aubrey. "Grasp it clearly yourself; then educate her up to a proper understanding of the matter. All of us who are worth anything in this world have lived before—not once, nor twice, but many times. We bring the varied experiences of all previous existences, unconsciously to bear upon and to enrich this one. Have you not often heard the expression 'A born musician'? What do we mean by that? Why, a man born with a knowledge, a sense, an experience, of music, who does not require to go through the mill of learning all the rudiments before music can express itself through him, because the soul of music is in him. He plays by instinct —some folk call it inspiration. Technical skill he may have to acquire—his fingers are new to it. The understanding of notation he may have to master again—the brain he uses *consciously* is also of fresh construction. But the subconscious self, the *Ego* of the man, the real eternal soul of him, leaps back with joy to the thing he has done perfectly before. He is a born musician; just as John the Baptist was a born prophet, because, into the little body prepared by Zacharias and Elisabeth, came the great *Ego* of Elijah reincarnate; to reappear as a full-grown prophet on the banks of the Jordan—the very spot from which he had been caught away, his life-work only half-accomplished, nine centuries before. Even our good Helen, if she knows her

Bible, could hardly question this, remembering Whom it was Who said: 'If ye will receive it, this *is* Elijah which was for to come; and they knew him not, but have done unto him whatsoever they listed.' "

"Great Scott!" exclaimed Ronnie. "What a theory! But indeed Helen would question it; and not only so, but she would be exceedingly upset and very much annoyed."

"Then Helen would fully justify the 'If' of the greatest of all teachers. She would come under the heading of those who refuse to receive a truth, however clearly and unmistakably expressed."

"Lor!" exclaimed Ronnie, in undisguised perplexity. "You have completely cornered me. But then I never set up for being a theologian."

"No, you are a born artist and musician. Music, tone, sound, colour, vibrate in every page of your romances. Had your parents taught you harmony, the piano, and the fiddle, your music would have burst forth along its normal lines. As they merely taught you the alphabet and grammar, your creative faculty turned to literature; you wrote romance full of music, instead of composing music full of romance. It is a distinction without a difference. But, now that you have found your mislaid 'cello, and I am teaching you to KNOW YOURSELF, you will do both."

Ronald stared across at Aubrey. His head was throbbing. Every moment he seemed to become more certain that he had indeed, many times before, held the Infant of Prague between his knees.

But there was a weird, uncanny feeling in the room. Helen seemed to walk in, to seat herself in the empty chair; and, leaning forward, to look at him steadily, with her clear earnest eyes. She seemed to repeat impressively: "Aubrey is not a good man, Ronnie. He is not a man you should trust."

"Well?" asked Aubrey, at last. "Do you recognise the truth?"

Then, with an effort, Ronnie answered as he believed Helen would have answered; and her face beside him, seemed to smile approval.

"It sounds a plausible theory," he said slowly; "it may possibly be a truth. But it is not a truth required by us now. Our obvious duty in the present is to live this life out to its fullest and best, regarding it as a time of preparation for the next."

Aubrey's thin lips framed the word "Rubbish!" but, checking it unuttered, substituted: "Quite right. This existence *is* a preparation for the next; just as that which preceded was a preparation for this."

Then Ronnie ceased to express Helen, and gave vent to an idea of his own.

"It would make a jolly old muddle of all our relationships," he said.

"Not at all," replied Aubrey. "It merely readjusts them, compensating for disappointments in the present, by granting us the assurance of past possessions, and the expectation of future enjoyment. In the life which preceded this, Helen was probably *my* wife, while *you* were a beautiful old person in diamond shoe-buckles, knee-breeches, and old lace, who played the 'cello at our wedding."

"Confound you!" cried Ronnie, in sudden fury, springing up and swinging the 'cello above his head, as if about to bring it down, with a crashing blow, upon Aubrey. "Damned old shoe-buckle yourself! Helen was never your wife! More likely you blacked her boots and mine!"

"Oh, hush!" smiled Aubrey, in contemptuous amusement. "Excellent young men who make innocent love in rose-gardens, never say 'damn.' And in those days, dear boy, we did not use shoe-blacking. Pray calm yourself, and sit down. You are upsetting the internal arrangements of your Infant. If you swing a baby violently about, it makes it sick. Any old Gamp will tell you that."

Ronnie sat down; but solely because his knees suddenly gave way beneath him. The floor on which he was standing seemed to become deep sand.

"Keep calm," sneered Aubrey Treherne. "Perhaps you would like to know my excellent warrant for concluding that Helen was my wife in a former life? She came very near to being my wife in this. She was engaged to me before she ever met you, my boy. Had it not been for the interference of that strong-minded shrew, Mrs. Dalmain, she would have married me. I had kissed my cousin Helen, as much as I pleased, before you had ever touched her hand."

The incandescent lights grew blood-red, leaping up and down, in wild, bewildering frolic.

Then they steadied suddenly. Helen's calm, lovely figure in a shaft of sunlight, reappeared in the empty chair.

Ronnie handed the Infant to her; rose, staggered across the intervening space, and struck Aubrey Treherne a violent blow on the mouth.

Aubrey gripped his arms, and for a moment the two men glared at one another.

Then Ronnie's knees gave way again; his feet sank deeply into the sand; and Aubrey, forcing him violently backward, pinned him down in his chair.

"I would kill you for this," he whispered, his face very close to Ronnie's; blood streaming from his lip. "I would kill you for this, you clown! But I mean to kiss Helen again; and life, while it holds that prospect, is too sweet to risk losing for the mere pleasure of wiping you out. Otherwise, I would kill you now, with my two hands."

Then a black pulsating curtain rolled, in impenetrable folds, between Ronnie and that livid bleeding face, and he sank away—down—down—down—into silent depths of darkness and of solitude.

CHAPTER VI

AUBREY PUTS DOWN HIS FOOT

RONNIE'S FIRST sensation as he returned to consciousness, was of extreme lassitude and exhaustion.

His eyelids lifted heavily; he had some difficulty in realising where he was.

Then he saw his 'cello, leaning against a chair; and, a moment later, Aubrey Treherne, lying back in the seat opposite, enveloped in a cloud of tobacco smoke.

"Hullo, West!" said Aubrey, kindly. "You put in your half-hour quite unexpectedly. You were trying, in a sleepy fashion, to tell me how you came to purchase this fine 'cello; but you dropped off, with the tale unfinished."

Ronnie looked in silence at his wife's cousin.

"Are you better for your sleep?"

"I am fagged out," said Ronnie, wearily.

Aubrey went to a cupboard, poured something into a glass, and handed it to Ronald.

"Drink this, my boy. It will soon wake you up."

Ronnie drank it. Its tint was golden, its odour, fragrant; but otherwise, for aught he knew, it might have been pure water.

He sat up and took careful note of his surroundings.

Then an idea seemed to strike him. He leaned forward and twanged the strings of his 'cello. They were not in tune.

"Will you lend me your tuning-fork?" he said to Aubrey.

But Aubrey had expected this.

"Sorry," he said. "I don't possess one, just now. I gave away mine last week. You can tune your 'cello by the organ."

"I don't know how to tune a 'cello," said Ronnie.

4

"Let me show you," suggested Aubrey, with the utmost friendliness.

He walked over to the organ, drew out the 'cello stop, sounded a note, then came back humming it.

Then he took up the Infant and carefully tuned the four strings, talking easily meanwhile.

"You see? You screw up the pegs—so. The notes are A, D, G, C."

"What have you done to your lip?" said Ronald, suddenly.

"Knocked it on the stove just now, as I bent to stoke it with my fingers, for fear of waking you. It bled amazingly."

Aubrey produced a much-stained handkerchief.

"It is curious how a tiny knock will sometimes draw as much blood as a sword-thrust. There! The Infant is in perfect tune, so far as I can tell without the bow. Do you mind if I just pass the bow across the strings? After each string is perfectly tuned to a piano or organ, you must make them vibrate together in order to get the fifths perfect. A violin or a 'cello is capable of a more complete condition of intuneness—if I may coin a word—than an organ or a piano."

He took up the bow, then with careful precision sounded the strings, singly and together. The beautiful open notes of the Infant of Prague, filled the room.

"There," said Aubrey, putting it back against the empty chair. "I am afraid that is all I must attempt. I only play the fiddle. I might disappoint you in your Infant if I did more than sound the open strings."

Ronald passed his hand over his forehead. "When did I fall asleep?" he asked.

"Just after suggesting that we should not discuss your books or your public."

"Ah, I remember! Treherne, I have had the most vivid and horrid nightmares."

"Then forget them," put in Aubrey, quickly. "Never recount a nightmare, when it is over. You suffer all its horrors again, in the telling. Turn your thoughts to something pleasant. When do you reach England?"

"I cross by the Hook, the day after to-morrow, reaching London early the following morning. I shall go to my club, see my publishers, lunch in town, and get down home to tea."

"To the moated Grange?" inquired Aubrey.

"Yes, to the Grange. Helen will await me there. But why do you call it 'moated'? We do not boast a moat."

Aubrey laughed. "I suppose my thoughts had run to 'Mariana.' You remember? 'He cometh not,' she said; the young woman who grew tired of waiting. They do, sometimes, you know! I believe *her* grange was moated. All granges should be moated; just as all old manors should be haunted. What a jolly time you and Helen must have in that lovely old place. I knew it well as a boy."

"You must come and stay with us," said Ronnie, with an effort.

"Thanks, dear chap, Delighted. Has Helen kept well during your absence?"

"Quite well. She wrote as often as she could, but there was a beastly long time when I could get no letters. Hullo! —I say!"

Ronnie stood up suddenly, the light of remembrance on his thin face, and began plunging his hands into the many pockets of his Norfolk coat.

"I found a letter from Helen at the *Poste Restante*, here; but owing to my absorption in the Infant, I clean forgot to read it! Heaven send I haven't dropped it anywhere!"

He stood with his back to the stove, hunting vaguely, but feverishly, in all his pockets.

Aubrey smoked on, watching him without stirring.

Aubrey was wishing that Helen could know how long

her letter had remained unread, owing to the Infant of Prague.

At length Ronnie found the letter—a large, square foreign envelope—safely stowed away in his pocket-book, in the inner breast-pocket of his coat.

"Of course," he said. "I remember. I put it there when I was writing Zimmermann's cheque. You will excuse me if I read it straight away? There may be something requiring a wire."

"Naturally, my dear fellow; read it. Cousins need not stand on ceremony; and the Infant now being thoroughly in tune, your mind is free to spare a thought or two to Helen. Don't delay another moment. There may be a message in the letter for me."

Ronnie drew the thin sheets from the envelope in feverish haste.

As he did so, a folded note fell from among them unseen by Ronnie, and dropped to the floor close to Aubrey's foot.

Ronnie began reading; but black spots danced before his eyes, and Helen's beautiful clear writing zig-zagged up and down the page.

Presently his vision cleared a little and he read more easily.

Suddenly he laughed, a short, rather mirthless, laugh.

"What's up?" inquired Aubrey Treherne.

"Oh, nothing much; only I suppose I'm in for a lecture again! Helen says: 'Ronald'——" Ronnie lifted his eyes from the paper. "What a nuisance it is to own that kind of name. As a small boy I was always 'Ronnie' when people were pleased, and 'Ronald' if I was in for a wigging. The feeling of it sticks to you all your life."

"Of course it does," said Aubrey sympathetically. "Beastly hard lines. Well? Helen says 'Ronald'——?"

Ronnie's eyes sought the paper again; but once more the

black spots danced in a wild shower. He rubbed his eyes and went on reading.

" 'Ronald, I shall have something to tell you when you get home, which will make a great difference to this Christmas, and to all Christmas-times to come. I will not put it into a letter. I will wait until you are here, and I can say it.' "

"What can it be?" questioned Aubrey.

"Oh, I know," said Ronnie, unsteadily—the floor was becoming soft and sandy again. "I have heard it all before. She always thinks me extravagant at Christmas, and objects to her old people being given champagne and other seasonable good things. I have heard—heard it—all before. There was no need to write about it. And when she—when she says it, I shall jolly well tell her that a—that a—a fellow can do as he likes with his own earnings."

"I should," said Aubrey Treherne.

Ronald went on reading, in silence.

Aubrey's eye was upon the folded sheet of paper on the floor.

Suddenly Ronnie said: "Hullo! I'm to have it after all! Listen to this. 'P.S.—On second thoughts, now you are so nearly home, I would rather you knew what I have to say, before you return; so I am enclosing with this a pencil note I wrote some weeks ago. *Ronnie, we will have a Christmas-tree this Christmas.*' Well, I never!" said Ronnie. "That's not a very wild thing in the way of extravagance, is it! But it's a concession. I have wanted a Christmas-tree each Christmas. But Helen said you couldn't have a Christmas-tree in a home where there were no kids; it was absurd for two grown up people to give each other a Christmas-tree. Now, where is——" He began searching in the empty envelope.

With a quick stealthy movement, Aubrey put his foot upon the note.

"It is not here," said Ronnie, shaking out the thin sheets

one by one, and tearing open the envelope. "She has forgotten it, after all. Well—I should think it will keep. It can hardly have been important."

"Evidently," remarked Aubrey, "third thoughts followed second thoughts. Even Helen would scarcely put a lecture on economy into a welcome-home letter."

"No, of course not," agreed Ronnie, and walked unsteadily to his chair.

Aubrey, stooping, transferred the note from beneath his foot to his pocket.

Ronald read his letter through again, then turned to Aubrey.

"Look here," he said. "I must send a wire. Helen wants to know whether I wish her to meet me in town, or whether I would rather she waited for me at home. What shall I say?"

Aubrey Treherne rose. "Think it over," he said, "while I fetch a form."

He left the room.

He was some time in finding that form.

When he returned his face was livid, his hand shook.

Ronald sat in absorbed contemplation of the Infant.

"It appears more perfect every time one sees it," he remarked, without looking at Aubrey.

Aubrey handed him a form for foreign telegrams, and a fountain-pen.

"What are you going to say to—to your wife?" he asked in a low voice.

"I don't know," said Ronnie, vaguely. "What a jolly pen! What am I to do with this?"

"You are to let Helen know whether she is to meet you in town, or to wait at the Grange."

"Ah, I remember. What do you advise, Treherne? I don't seem able to make plans."

"I should say most decidedly, let her wait for you at home."

"Yes, I think so too. I shall be rushing around in town. I can get home before tea-time. How shall I word it?"

"Why not say: *Owing to satisfactory news in letter, prefer to meet you quietly at home. All well.*"

Ronnie wrote this at Aubrey's dictation; then he paused.

"What news?" he asked, perplexed at the words he himself had written.

"Why—that Helen is quite well. Isn't that satisfactory news?"

"Oh, of course. I see. Yes?"

"Then you might add: *Will wire train from London.*"

"But I know the train now," objected Ronnie. "I have been thinking of it for weeks! I shall catch the 3 o'clock express."

"Very well, then add: *Coming by 3 o'clock train. Home to tea.*"

Ronnie wrote it—a joyous smile on his lips and in his eyes.

"It sounds so near," he said. "After seven long months —it sounds so near!"

"Now," said Aubrey, "give it to me. I will take it out for you. I know an office where one can hand in wires at any hour."

"You *are* a good fellow," said Ronnie gratefully.

"And now look here," continued Aubrey. "Before I go, you must turn into bed, old chap. You need sleep more than you know. I can do a little prescribing myself. I am going to give you a dose of sleeping stuff which brought me merciful oblivion, after long nights of maddening wakefulness. You will feel another man, when you wake in the morning. But I am coming with you to The Hague. I can tend the Infant, while you go to the publishers. I will see you safely on board at the Hook, on the following evening, and next day you will be at home. After all those months alone in the long grass, you don't want any more solitary travelling. Now come to bed."

Ronnie rose unsteadily. "Aubrey," he said, "you are a

most awfully good fellow. I shall tell Helen. She will—will—will be so—so grateful. I'm perfectly all right, you know; but other people seem so—so busy, and—and—so vague. You will help me to—to—to—arrest their attention. I must take the Infant to bed."

"Yes, yes," said Aubrey; "we will find a cosy place for the Infant. If Helen were here she would provide a bassinet. Don't forget that joke. It will amuse Helen. I make you a present of it. *If Helen were here she would provide a bassinet and a pram for the Infant of Prague.*"

Ronnie laughed. "I shall tell Helen you said so." Then, carrying the 'cello, he lurched unsteadily through the doorway. The Infant's head had a narrow escape.

Aubrey Treherne sent off the telegram. He required to alter only one word.

When it reached Helen, the next morning at breakfast, it read thus: *Owing to astonishing news in letter, prefer to meet you quietly at home. All well. Coming by 3 o'clock train. Home to tea.—Ronald.*

Helen suffered a sharp pang of disappointment. She had expected something quite different. The adjective "astonishing" seemed strangely cold and unlike Ronnie. She had thought he would say "wonderful," or "unbelievable," or "glorious."

But before she had finished her first cup of coffee, she had reasoned herself back into complete content. Ronnie, in an unusual fit of thoughtfulness, had remembered her feeling about the publicity of telegrams. She had so often scolded him for putting "darling" and "best of love" into messages which all had to be shouted by telephone from the postal town, into the little village office which, being also the village grocery store, was a favourite rendezvous at all hours of the day for village gossips.

It was quite unusually considerate of Ronnie to curb the

glowing words he must have longed to pour forth. The very effort of that curbing, had reduced him to a somewhat stilted adjective.

So Helen finished her lonely breakfast with thoughts of glad anticipation. Ronnie's return was drawing so near. Only two more breakfasts without him. At the third she would be pouring out his coffee, and hearing him comment on the excellence of Blake's hot buttered toast!

Then, with a happy heart, she went up to the nursery.

Yet—unconsciously—the pang remained.

CHAPTER VII

A FRIEND IN NEED

As AUBREY TREHERNE, on his way back from dispatching the telegram, stood in the general entrance hall, fumbling with the latchkey at the door of his own flat, a tall young man in an ulster dashed up the wide stone stairs, rapidly read the names on the various brass plates, and arrived at Aubrey's just as his door had yielded to persuasion and was admitting him into his own small passage.

"Hullo," said a very British voice. "Do you happen to be Ronald West's wife's cousin?"

Aubrey turned in the doorway, taking stock of his interlocutor. He saw a well-knit, youthful figure, a keen resourceful face, and a pair of exceedingly bright brown eyes, unwavering in the steady penetration of their regard. Already they had taken him in, from top to toe, and were looking past him in a rapid investigation of as much of his flat as could be seen from the doorway.

Aubrey was caught!

He had fully intended muffling his electric bell, and not being at home to visitors.

But this brisk young man, with an atmosphere about him of always being ten minutes ahead of time, already had one of his very muddy boots inside the door, and eagerly awaited the answer to his question; so it was useless to reply to the latter in German, and to bang the former.

Therefore: "I have that honour," replied Aubrey, with the best grace he could muster.

"Ah! Well, I'm sorry to bother you so late, but I must have a word with you; and then I am going round to spend the night with Ronnie at his hotel."

"Come in," said Aubrey, in a low voice; "but we must not talk in the passage or we shall wake him. I saw he was not fit to be alone, so I sent to the hotel for his traps, and am putting him up here. He turned in, half an hour ago, and seemed really inclined to sleep. He was almost off, when I left him."

Aubrey, closing the door, led the way to his sitting-room, where the three easy chairs were still drawn up before the stove.

"I conclude you are Dr. Cameron," said Aubrey, turning up the light, and motioning his visitor to the chair which had lately been Ronnie's.

"Yes, I am Dick Cameron, Ronnie's particular chum; and if ever he needed a particular chum, poor old chap, he does so at this moment. But I am glad he has found a friend in you, and one really able to undertake him. You did right not to leave him at the hotel; and he must not travel back to England alone."

"I have already arranged to accompany him," said Aubrey Treherne.

"Good; it will save me a journey."

Dick pulled off his ulster, threw it across the red velvet sofa, flung his cap after it, and took the proffered chair.

In his blue serge suit and gay tie, he looked like the captain of a college football team.

Aubrey, eyeing him with considerable reserve and distaste, silently took up his position in the chair opposite. He felt many years older than this peremptory young man, who appeared to consider himself master of all situations.

Dick turned his bright eyes on to the empty chair between them.

"So Ronnie has spent the evening with you?"

"He has."

"Who was the third party?"

"The third party was the Infant of Prague."

"Oh, bother that rotten Infant!" exclaimed Dr. Dick. "I came near to putting my foot through its shining tummy this morning! Still it may serve its silly use, if it takes his mind off his book, until we can get him safely home. I suppose you know, sir, that Ronald West is about as ill as a man can be? It will be touch and go whether we can get him home before the crash comes."

"I thought he seemed excited and unwell," said Aubrey. "What do you consider is the cause of his condition?"

"Well, the bother is, we can't exactly tell. But I should say he has been letting himself in for constant exposure to extreme heat by day, and to swampy dampness by night; not taking proper food; living in a whirl of excited imagination with no rational companionship to form an outlet; and on the top of all this, contracted some malarial germ, which has put up his temperature and destroyed the power of natural sleep. This condition of brain has enabled him to work practically night and day at his manuscript, and I have no doubt he has written brilliant stuff, which an enchanted world will read by and by, with no notion of the price which has been paid for their pleasure and edification. But meanwhile, unless proper steps are taken to avert disaster, our friend Ronnie will be, by then, unable to understand or to enjoy his triumph."

Aubrey's lean face flushed. "I hope you are taking an exaggerated view," he said.

"I hope you understand," retorted Dr. Dick, "that I am doing nothing of the kind. I cannot tell you precisely what course the illness will run; the nuisance of these African jungle poisons is that we know precious little about them. But I have known Ronnie since he and I were at school together, and any poison goes straight to his brain. If he gets influenza, he never sneezes and snuffles like an ordinary mortal, but walks about, more or less light-headed, all day; and lies dry awake, staring at the ceiling all night."

"What do you recommend in this case?"

"Ah, there we arrive at my reason for coming to you. I don't know Ronnie's wife. I conclude *you* do."

"She is my first cousin. I have known her intimately all her life."

"Can you write to her to-night, and mail the letter so that it will reach her before he arrives home?"

"I have every intention of doing so."

Dick Cameron sat forward, eagerly.

"Good! It will come better from you than from a total stranger. No doubt I am known to her by name; but we have never chanced to meet. Without alarming her too much, I want you to make Ronnie's condition quite clear to her. Tell her he must be kept absolutely quiet and happy on his return; and, with as little delay as may be, she must have the best advice procurable."

"Whom would you recommend?"

"To be quite honest, I am afraid a brain specialist. But I will give you the name of a man who has also made a special study of the conditions caused by malarial fever, and exposure to tropical heat."

Dick produced a note-book, wrote down a name and address, tore out the leaf, and handed it to Aubrey.

"There! You can't do better than that. Of course it is

everything that you are taking him right home. But, even so, let your letter get there first. You might have difficulty in seeing Mrs. West alone, and mischief might be done in a moment, which you would be powerless to prevent. Tell her, that above all else, she must avoid any sort of shock for him. A violent emotion of any kind would probably send send him clean off his head."

"I am sure you are right, there," said Aubrey. "He suddenly became violent to-night, while we were talking about his 'cello; got up, staggered across, and struck me on the mouth."

Dr. Dick's keen eyes were instantly bent upon Aubrey Treherne in perplexed scrutiny.

Aubrey shifted uncomfortably in his seat; then rose and put fuel into the stove.

Still Dick sat silent.

When Aubrey resumed his seat, Dick spoke—slowly, as if carefully weighing every word.

"Now that is peculiar," he said. "Ronnie's mental condition is a perfectly amiable one, unless anything was said or done to cause him extreme provocation. In fact, he would not be easily provoked. He is inclined rather to take a maudlinly affectionate and friendly view of things and people; to be very simple, almost childishly, pleased with the last new idea. That wretched Infant of his, is a case in point. I should be glad if you would tell me, sir, what happened in this room just before Ronnie hit out."

"Merely a conversation about the 'cello," replied Aubrey, hurriedly. "A perfectly simple remark of mine apparently annoyed him. But I soon pacified him. He was obviously not responsible for his actions."

"He was obviously in a frenzy of rage," remarked Dr. Dick, dryly; "and he caught you a good one on the mouth. Did he apologise afterwards?"

"He fell asleep," said Aubrey, "and appeared on awakening to have absolutely forgotten the occurrence."

Dick got up, put his hands in his pockets, walked over to the organ, and, bending down, examined the stops. He whistled softly to himself as he did so.

Aubrey, meanwhile, had the uncomfortable sensation that the whole scene with Ronnie was being re-acted, with Dick Cameron as an interested spectator.

It tried Aubrey's nerves.

"I do not wish to hurry you," he suggested presently. "But if I am to post my letter to my cousin before midnight, the sooner I am able to write it, the better."

Dick turned at once and took up his ulster.

Aubrey relieved, came forward cordially to lend him a hand.

"No, thank you," said Dr. Dick. "A man should always get into his coat unaided. In so doing, he uses certain muscles which are exercised in no other way."

He swung himself into the heavy coat, and stood before Aubrey Treherne—very tall, very grave, very determined.

"You quite understand, sir, that if you were not yourself taking Ronnie home, I should do so? And if, by any chance, you are prevented from going, just let me know, and I can be packed and ready to start home with him in a quarter of an hour."

"Very good of you," said Aubrey, "but all our plans are made. We reach The Hague to-morrow night. He requires a day there for making his translation and publishing arrangements. So we sleep at The Hague to-morrow, crossing by the Hook of Holland on the following evening. I have wired to the Hôtel des Indes for a suite. I feel sure my cousin would wish him to have the best of everything, and to be absolutely comfortable and quiet. At the Hôtel des Indes they have an excellent orchestra, and a particularly fine 'cellist. West will enjoy showing him the Infant. They can compare babies! It will keep him amused and interested all the evening."

"Good idea," agreed Dr. Dick. "But Ronnie need not come down on his wife for his hotel expenses! He is making a pot of money himself, now. You will be careful to report to Mrs. West exactly what I have said of his condition?"

"I will write immediately. As we stay a night *en route*, and another is taken up in crossing, my cousin should receive my letter twenty-four hours before our arrival."

"Impress upon her," said Dr. Dick, earnestly, "how dangerous any mental shock might be."

"Do you fear brain fever?" questioned Aubrey.

Dick laughed. "Brain fever is a popular fiction," he said. "It is not a term admitted by the faculty. If you mean meningitis—no, I trust not. But probably temporary loss of memory, and a complete upsetting of mental control; with a possible impairing, for a considerable time, of his brilliant mental powers."

"In other words, my cousin's husband is threatened with insanity."

"Lor, no!" exclaimed Dick, with vehemence. "How easily you good people hand a fellow-creature over to that darkest of all fates! Ronnie's condition is brought about by temporary circumstances which are not in the least likely to have permanent results. He has always had the eccentricity of genius; but, since his genius has been recognised, people have ceased to consider him eccentric. Now I must be off. But I will see him first. Will you show me his room?"

"He is asleep," objected Aubrey. "Is it not a pity to disturb him?"

"I doubt his being asleep," replied Dick. "But if he is, we shall not wake him."

He stepped into the passage, his attitude one of uncompromising determination.

Aubrey Treherne opened the door of Ronnie's room. It was in darkness. He stepped back into the passage, lighted a candle, handed it to Dick Cameron, and they entered quietly together.

Ronnie lay on his back, sleeping heavily. His eyes were partly open, his face flushed, his breathing rapid. One arm was flung out towards a chair beside the bed, on which lay his pocket-book, his watch, and a small leather miniature-case containing a portrait of Helen. This lay open upon the watch, having evidently fallen from his fingers. A candle had burned down into the socket, and spluttered itself out.

Dick picked up the miniature, held it close to the light of his own candle, and examined it critically.

"He certainly went in for beauty," he remarked in a low voice to Aubrey Treherne, as he laid the miniature beside the pocket-book. "Of course Ronnie would. But it is also a noble face—a face one could altogether trust. Ronnie will be in safe hands when once you get him home."

Aubrey's smile, in the flare of the candle, was the grin of a hungry wolf. He made no reply.

Dr. Dick, watch in hand, stood silently beside the bed, counting the rapid respiration of his friend. Then he turned, took up an empty tumbler from the table behind him, smelt it, and looked at Aubrey Treherne.

"I thought so," he said. "You meant well, no doubt. But don't do it again. Drugs to produce sleep may occasionally be necessary, but should only be given under careful medical supervision. Personally, I am inclined to think that any sort of artificial sleep does more harm to a delicately poised brain, than insomnia. However, opinions differ. But there is no question that your experiment of to-night must not be repeated. I have given him stuff to take during his homeward journey which will tend to calm him, lessen the fever, and clear his mind. See that he takes it."

Young Dick Cameron walked out of Ronnie's room, blew out the candle he carried, and replaced the candlestick on a little ornamental bracket.

Aubrey followed, inwardly fuming.

If Dick had been at the top of the tree, the first opinion procurable from Harley Street, W., his manner could hardly have been more authoritative, his instructions more peremptory.

"Upstart!" said Aubrey to himself. "Insolent Jackanapes!"

When Dick Cameron reached the outer door his cap was on the back of his head, his hands were thrust deep into his coat pockets.

"Good evening," he said. "Excuse my long intrusion. I shall be immensely obliged if you will let me have a wire reporting your safe arrival, and a letter, later on, with details as to Ronnie's state. I put my address on the paper I gave you just now, with the name of the man Mrs. West must call in."

Dick crossed the great entrance-hall, and ran lightly down the stone steps.

Aubrey heard the street door close behind him.

Then he shut and double locked his own flat.

"Upstart!" he said. "Jackanapes! Insolent fool!"

It is sometimes consoling to call people that which you know they are not, yet heartily wish they were.

Aubrey entered his sitting-room. He wanted an immediate vent for his ill-humour and sense of impotent mortification.

The leaf from Dick's note-book lay on the table.

Aubrey took it up, opened the iron door of the stove, and thrust the leaf into the very heart of the fire.

CHAPTER VIII

PARADISE LOST

Aubrey Treherne sat at his writing-table, his head buried in his hands.

Before him lay the closely-written sheets of his letter to Helen; beside them her pencil note which had fallen, unnoticed by Ronnie, from her letter to him.

Presently Aubrey lifted his head. His face bore traces of the anguish of soul through which he had been passing.

A man who has yielded himself to unrestrained wrongdoing, suffers with a sharpness of cold misery unknown to the brave true heart, however hard or lonely may be his honourable way.

Before finally reading his own letter to Helen, Aubrey read again her pathetic note to her husband.

"Ronnie, my own!

"Excuse pencil and bad writing. Nurse has propped me up in bed, but not so high as I should like.

"Darling, I am not ill, only rather weak, and very, very happy.

"Ronnie, I must write to you on this first day of being allowed a pencil, though I shall not, of course, yet send the letter. In fact, I dare say I shall keep it, and give it to you by and by. But you will like to feel that I wrote at once.

"Darling, how shall I tell you? Beside me, in your empty place, as I write, lies your little son—our own baby boy, Ronnie!

"He came three days ago.

"Oh, Ronnie, it is so wonderful! He is *so* like you; though his tiny fingers are all pink and crinkled, and his palms are like little sea-shells. But he is going to have your artistic hands. When I cuddle them against my neck, the awful longing and loneliness of these past months seem wiped out. But only because he is yours, darling, and because I know you are soon coming back to him and to me.

"I could not tell you before you went, because I know you would have felt obliged to give up going, and your book is so important; and I have not told you since, because you must not have anything to worry you while so far away. Also I was glad to bear it alone, and to save you the hard part. One soon forgets the hardness, in the joy.

"Jane was with me.

"We are sending no announcement to the papers, for fear you should see it on the way home. Very few people know.

"Our little son will be six weeks old, when you get back. I shall be quite strong again.

"I hope you will be able to read this tiny writing. Nurse would only give me one sheet of paper!

"His eyes are blue. His little mouth is just like yours. I kiss it, but it doesn't kiss back! He is a darling, Ronnie, but—he isn't you!

"Come back soon, to your more than ever loving wife,

"HELEN.

"Yes, the smudgy places *are* tears, but only because I am rather weak, and so happy."

Crossing the first page came a short postscript, in firmer handwriting:

"After all I am sending this to Leipzig. I daren't not tell you before you arrive. I sometimes feel as if I had done something wrong! Tell me, directly you take me in your arms, that I did right, and that you are glad. I am down, as usual, now, and baby is quite well."

Aubrey's hands shook as he folded the thin paper, opened a drawer, pushed the letter far into it, and locked the drawer.

Then, with set face, he turned to his own letter to Ronald West's wife.

"My own Beloved—

"Yes, I call you so still, because you *were* mine, and *are* mine. You threw me over, giving me no chance to prove that my love for you had made me worthy—that I would have been worthy. You sent me into outer darkness, where there was wailing and gnashing of teeth; where the worm of remorse dies—never. But, through it all, I loved you still. I love you to-night, as I never loved you before. The whole world is nothing to me, excepting as the place on which you walk.

"I have seen the man—the selfish, self-absorbed fool—on whom you threw yourself away, six months after you had cast me adrift. At this moment he is my guest, snoring in an adjoining room while I sit up writing to you.

"He has spent the evening talking of nothing but himself, his journey, his wonderful book—the strongest thing he has done yet, etc., etc., etc.; till I could have risen up and strangled him with my two hands. Oh, Helen—my lovely one—he is altogether unworthy of you! I saw a letter of yours long ago, in which you said he was like a young sun-god. Handsome he is, I admit. He says he has never felt fitter in his life, and he looks it. But surely a woman wants more than mere vitality and vigour and outward beauty of appearance? Heart—he has none. The wonderful news in your letter has left him unmoved. He thinks more of a 'cello he has just bought, than he does of your little son. When I remonstrated with him, he rose up and struck me on the mouth. But I forgave him for your sake, and he now sleeps under my roof.

"Helen, he *must* have disappointed you over and over again. He will continue to disappoint you.

"Helen, you loved me once; and when a woman loves once, she loves for always.

"Helen, if he could leave you alone during seven months, in order to get local scenery for a wretched manuscript, he will leave you again, and again, and yet again. He married you for your money; he has practically admitted it to me; but now that he is making a yearly income larger than your own, he has no more use for you.

"Oh, my beloved—my queen—my only Love—don't stay with a man who is altogether unworthy of you! If a man disappoints a woman she has a right to leave him. He is not what she believed him to be; that fact sets her free. If you had found out, afterwards, that he was already married to another, would you not have left him? Well, he *was* already wedded to himself and to his career. He had no whole-hearted devotion to give to you.

"Helen, don't wait for his return. Directly you get this come out here to me. Bring your little son and his nurse. My flat will be absolutely at your disposal. I can sleep elsewhere; and I swear to you I will never stay one moment after you have bid me go. As soon as West has set you legally free, we can marry and travel abroad for a couple of years; then, when the whole thing has blown over, go back to live in the old house so dear to us both.

"Helen, you will have twenty-four hours in which to get away before he returns. But even if you decide to await his return, it will not be too late. His utter self-absorption must give you a final disillusion.

"See if his first words to you are not about his cursed 'cello, rather than about his child and yours.

"If so, treat him with the silent contempt he deserves, and come at once to the man who won you first and to whom you have always belonged; come, where tenderest consideration and the worship of a lifetime await you.

"Yours till death—and after,

"Aubrey Treherne."

CHAPTER IX

THE PINNACLE OF THE TEMPLE

AUBREY'S LETTER fell upon Helen as a crushing, stunning blow.

At first her womanhood reeled beneath it.

"What have I been—what have I done," she cried, "that a man dares to write thus to me?"

Then her wifehood rose up in arms as she thought of Ronnie's gay, boyish trust in her; their happy life together; his joyous love and laughter.

She clenched her hands.

"I could *kill* Aubrey Treherne!" she said.

Then her motherhood arose; and bowing her proud head, she burst into a passion of tears.

At length she stood up and walked over to the window.

"It will be bad for my little son if I weep," she said, and smiled through her tears.

The trees were leafless, the garden beds empty. The park looked sodden, dank and cheerless. Summer was long dead and over, yet frosts had not begun, bringing suggestions of mistletoe and holly.

But the mists were lifting, fading in white wreaths from off the grass; and, at that moment, the wintry sun, bursting through the November clouds, shone on the diamond panes, illumining the cross and the motto beneath it.

"*In hoc vince!*" murmured Helen. "As I told my own dear boy, the path of clear shining is the way to victory. *In hoc signo vinces!* I will take this gleam of sunlight as a token of triumph. By the help of God, I will write such an answer to Aubrey as shall lead him to overcome his evil desires, and bring his dark soul out into the light of repentance and confession."

The same post had brought her a short letter from Ronnie,

written immediately on his arrival at Leipzig, evidently before receiving hers. It was a disappointment to have nothing more. As Aubrey had got a letter through after hearing the news, Ronnie might have done the same.

But perhaps, face to face with her wonderful tidings, words had altogether failed him. He feared to spoil all he would so soon be able to say, by attempting to write.

To-morrow—the day which should bring him to her would soon be here.

Meanwhile her reply to Aubrey must be posted to-day, and his letter consigned to the flames.

Feeling unable to go to the nursery with that letter unanswered, she sat down at once and wrote to her cousin.

"I only read your letter, Aubrey, half an hour ago. I am answering it at once, because I cannot enter the presence of my little son, with such a letter as yours still in my possession. As soon as I have answered it I shall burn it.

"I may then be able to rise above the terrible sense of shame which completely overwhelmed me at first, at the thought that any man—above all a man who knew me well—should dare to write me such a letter!

"At first my whole soul cried out in horror: 'What am I? What have I been? What have I done—that such words should be written—such a proposition made—to me?' The sin of it seemed to soil me; the burning wickedness, to brand me. I seemed parted from my husband and my child, and dragged down with you into your abyss of outer darkness.

"Then, into my despair, sacred words were whispered for my comfort. 'He was in all points tempted, like as we are, *yet without sin*,' and, through my shame and tears, I saw a vision of the Holy One, standing serene and kingly on the pinnacle of the temple, where, though the devil dared to whisper the fiendish suggestion: 'Cast Thyself down,' He stood His ground without a tremor—tempted, yet unsoiled.

"So—with this vision of my Lord before me—I take my stand, Aubrey Treherne, upon the very summit of the holy temple of wifehood and motherhood, and I say to you: 'Get thee gone, Satan!' You may have bowed my mind to the very dust in shame over your wicked words, but you cannot cause my womanhood to descend one step from off its throne.

"This being so, poor Aubrey, I feel able to forgive you the other great wrong, and to try to find words in which to prove to you the utter vileness of the sin, and yet to show you also the way out of your abyss of darkness and despair, into the clear shining of repentance, confession, and forgiveness.

"As regards the happenings of the past, between you and me—you state them wrongly. I did not love you, Aubrey, or I would never have sent you away. I could have forgiven anything to an honest man, who had merely failed and fallen.

"But you had lived a double life; you had deceived me all along the line. I had loved the man I thought you were—the man you had led me to believe you were. I did not love the man I found you out to be.

"I could not marry a man I did not love. Therefore, I sent you away. There was no question then of giving you, or not giving you, a chance to prove yourself worthy. I was not concerned just then with what you might eventually prove yourself. I did not love you: therefore, I could not wed you. Though, as a side issue, it is only fair to point out—if you wish to stand upon your possible merits—that this letter, written four years later, confirms my then estimate of your true character.

"Aubrey, I cannot discuss my husband with you; nor can I bring myself to allude to the subject of my relations with him, or his with me.

"To defend him to you, would be to degrade him in all honest eyes.

"To enlarge upon my love for him, would be like pouring crystal water into a stagnant polluted pool, in order to prove how pure was the fountain from which that water flowed. Nothing could be gained by such a proceeding. Pouring samples of its purity into the tainted waters of the pool, would neither prove the former, nor cleanse the latter.

"But, in order to free my own mind from the poison of your suggestions and the shame of the fact that they were made to me, I must answer, in the abstract, one statement in your letter. Please understand that I answer it completely in the abstract. You have dared to apply it to my husband and to me. I do not admit that it applies. But, even if it did, I should not let it pass unchallenged. I break a lance with you, Aubrey Treherne, and with all men of your way of thinking, on behalf of every true wife and mother in Christendom!

"You say, that if a man has disappointed his wife, she has a right to leave him; the fact of that disappointment sets her free?

"I say to you, in answer: when a woman loves a man enough to wed him, he becomes to her as her life—her very self.

"I often fail, and fall, and disappoint myself. I do not thereupon immediately feel free to commit suicide. I face my failure, resolve to do better, and take up my life again, as bravely as may be, on higher lines.

"If a woman leaves her husband she commits moral suicide. By virtue of his union with her, he is as her own self. If disappointment and disillusion come to her through him, she must face them as she does when they come through herself. She must be patient, faithful, understanding, tender; helping him, as she would help herself, to start afresh on higher ground; once more, with a holy courage, facing life bravely.

"This is my answer—every true woman's answer—to the subtle suggestions of your letter.

"I admit that often marriages turn out hopeless—impossible; mere prisons of degradation. But that is when the sacred tie is entered into for other than the essential reasons of a perfect love and mutual need; or without due consideration, 'unadvisedly, lightly, wantonly,' notwithstanding the Church's warning. Or when people have found out their mistake in time, yet lacked the required courage to break their engagement, as I broke off mine with you, Aubrey; thus saving you and myself a lifetime of regret and misery.

"Oh, cannot you see that the only real 'outer darkness' is the doing of wrong? Disappointment, loss, loneliness, remorse—all these may be hard to bear, but they can be borne in the light; they do not necessarily belong to the outer darkness.

"May I ask you, as some compensation for the pain your letter has given me, and the terrible effort this answer has cost, to bear with me if, in closing, I quote to you in full the final words of the first chapter of the first epistle of St. John? I do so with my heart full of hope and prayer for you—yes, even for you, Aubrey. Because, though *my* words will probably fail to influence you, God has promised that *His* Word shall never return unto Him void.

" 'If we walk in the light, as He is in the light, we have fellowship one with another, and the blood of Jesus Christ His Son cleanseth us from all sin. . . . If we confess our sins, He is faithful and just to forgive us our sins, and to cleanse us from all unrighteousness.'

"Oh, Aubrey, act on this! It is true.

"Your cousin, who still hopes better things of you, and who will not fail in thought and prayer,

"HELEN WEST."

PART III

CHAPTER X

RONNIE ARRIVES IN A FOG

RONNIE REACHED Liverpool Street Station at 8 o'clock on a foggy November morning.

After the quiet night on the steamer, the landing in darkness at Harwich, and the steady run up to town, alone in a first-class compartment, he felt momentarily confused by the noise and movement within the great city terminus.

The brilliant lights of the station, combined with the yellow fog rolling in from the various entrances; the onward rush of many feet, as hundreds of busy men and eager young women poured out of suburban trains, hurrying to the scenes which called for their energy during the whole of the coming day; the gliding in and out of trains, the passing to and fro of porters, wheeling heavy luggage; the clang of milk-cans, the hoot of taxi-cabs, and, beyond it all, the distant roar of London, awaking, and finding its way about heavily, like an angry old giant in the fog—all seemed to Ronnie to be but another of the queer nightmares which came to him now with exhausting frequency.

As a rule, he found it best to wait until they passed off. So, holding the Infant of Prague in its canvas case in one hand, and the bag containing his manuscript in the other, he stood quite still upon the platform, waiting for the roar to cease, the rush to pass by, and the nightmare to be over.

Presently an inspector who knew Ronnie, walked down the platform. He paused at once, with the ready and attentive courtesy of the London railway official.

"Any luggage, Mr. West?" he asked, lifting his cap.

"No, thank you," replied Ronnie, "not to-day."

He knew he had luggage somewhere—heaps of it. But what was the good of hunting up luggage in a nightmare? Dream luggage was not worth retrieving. Besides, the more passive you are, the sooner the delusion leaves off tormenting you.

"Have you come from the Hook, sir?" inquired the inspector.

"Yes," said Ronnie. "Did you think I had come from the Eye?"

He knew it was a vile pun, but it seemed exactly the sort of thing one says in a nightmare.

The inspector laughed, and passed on; then returned, looking rather searchingly at Ronnie.

Ronnie thought it well to explain further. "As a matter of fact, my friend," he said, "I have come from Central Africa, where I have been sitting round camp-fires, in company with asps and cockatrices, and other interesting creatures. I am writing a book about it—the best thing I have done yet."

The inspector had read and enjoyed all Ronnie's books. He smiled uneasily. Asps and cockatrices, sounded queer company.

"Won't you have a cup of coffee, sir, before going out into the fog?" he suggested.

"Ah—good idea!" said Ronnie; and made his way to the refreshment-room.

It was empty at this early hour, and quiet. All the people with rushing feet and vaguely busy faces had breakfasted at a still earlier hour, in their own cosy homes. Their wives had made their coffee. To-morrow Helen would pour out his coffee. It seemed an almost unbelievably happy thought. How came such rapture to be connected with coffee?

He spent a minute or two in deciding at which of the many little marble tables he would sit. He never remembered being offered so large or so varied a choice at Liverpool Street Station before. You generally made a dash for the only empty table you saw, usually close to the door. That was like Hobson's choice—this or none! A stable of forty good steeds, always ready and fit for travelling, but the customer must take the horse which stood nearest to the door!

Well, to-day he had the run of the stable. Forty good marble tables! Which should he choose?

The young woman behind the counter watched him with interest as he wandered about, carefully examining each table and sitting down tentatively at several. At last he chose the most central, as being the farthest removed from Hobson's choice; sat down, took the Infant out of its bag, and, screwing in its pointed foot, leaned it up against another chair at the table.

Then he found that one of the young women had come from behind the counter, and was standing at his elbow, patiently awaiting his pleasure.

He ordered a cup of coffee and a roll and butter, for himself; a glass of milk and a sponge-cake, for the Infant.

Just after these were served, before he had had time to drink the steaming hot coffee, the friendly inspector arrived, accompanied by another railway official. They said they had come to make sure Ronnie had found what he wanted in the refreshment-room.

Ronnie thanked them for their civility, and showed them the Infant.

They looked at it with surprise and interest; but nudged one another when they noticed the glass of milk and the sponge-cake, which Ronnie had carefully pushed across to the Infant's side of the table.

Then they saluted, and went out.

Left alone, Ronnie drank his coffee.

It instantly cleared his brain of the after-effects of the sleeping draught which Aubrey had insisted upon giving him just before the steamer sailed the night before. His surroundings ceased to appear dream-like. A great wave of happiness swept over him.

Why, he was in London again! He was almost at home! If he had let Helen meet him, she might have been sitting just opposite, at this little marble table!

He looked across and saw the unconscious Infant's glass of milk and sponge-cake. He drew them hurriedly towards him. He felt suddenly ashamed of them. It was possible to carry a joke too far in public. He knew Helen would say: "Don't be silly, Ronnie!"

He particularly disliked milk, and was not fond of sponge cakes; but he hastily drank the one, and ate the other. He could think of no other way of disposing of them. He hoped the young women who were watching him from behind the counter, would think he enjoyed them.

Then he called for a whisky and soda, to take out the exceedingly beastly taste of the milk; but instantly remembered that old Dick had said: "Touch no alcohol," so changed the order to another cup of coffee.

This second instalment of coffee made him feel extraordinarily fit and vigorous.

He put the Infant back into its bag.

The inspector returned.

"We have found your luggage, Mr. West," he said. "If we may have your keys we can get it out for you."

"Ah, do!" said Ronnie. "Many thanks. Put it on a taxi. I shall leave it at my club. I am afraid I was rather vague about it just now; but I had been given a sleeping-draught on board, and was hardly awake when I got out of the train. I am all right now, Thanks for your help, my good fellow."

The inspector looked relieved.

Ronnie paid his bill, took up the 'cello, handed his bag to the inspector, and marched off gaily to claim his luggage.

He felt like conquering the world! The fog was lifting. The roar of the city sounded more natural. He had an excellent report to make to his publisher, heaps of "copy" to show him, and then—he was going home to Helen.

In the taxi he placed the Infant on the seat beside him.

On the whole he felt glad he had told Helen not to meet him at the station. It was so much more convenient to have plenty of room in the taxi for his 'cello. It stood so safely on the seat beside him, in its canvas bag.

As they sped westward he enjoyed looking out at the fog and mud and general wintry aspect of London.

He did not feel cold. Aubrey had persuaded him to buy a magnificent fur-coat at The Hague. He had lived in it ever since, feeling gorgeous and cosy. Aubrey's ideas of spending money suited him better than Helen's.

His taxi glided rapidly along the greasy Embankment. Once it skidded on the tramlines, and Ronnie laid a steadying hand upon the 'cello.

The grey old Thames went rolling by—mighty, resistless, perpetually useful—right through the heart of busy London.

Ronnie thought of the well-meaning preacher who pointed out to his congregation, as an instance of the wonderful overrulings of an All-wise Providence, the fact that large rivers flowed through great cities, and small streams through little villages! Ronnie laughed very much at the recollection of this story, and tried to remember whether he had ever told it to Helen.

Arrived at his club he shaved, tubbed, changed his clothes, and, leaving his 'cello in charge of the hall porter, sallied out with his manuscript to call upon his publisher.

In his portmanteau he had found Dr. Dick's bottle of stuff to take on the journey. Aubrey had persuaded him to pack it away. He now took a dose; then slipped the bottle into the pocket of his fur coat.

All went well, during the rest of the morning. His

publisher was neither preoccupied nor vague. He gave Ronnie a great reception and his full attention.

In the best of spirits, and looking the bronzed picture of perfect health, Ronnie returned to his club, lunched, showed his 'cello to two or three friends, then caught the three o'clock train to Hollymead.

The seven months were over. All nightmares seemed to have cleared away. He was on his way to Helen. In an hour and a half he would be with her!

He began to wonder, eagerly, what Helen would say to the Infant.

He felt quite sure that as soon as he got the bow in his hand, and the 'cello between his knees, the Infant would have plenty to say to Helen.

He had kept his yearning to play, under strong control, so that she might be there to enjoy with him the wonderful experience of those first moments.

As the train slowed up for Hollymead, and the signal lights of the little wayside station appeared, Ronnie took the last dose of Dick's physic, and threw the bottle under the seat.

CHAPTER XI

THE MIRAGE

HELEN AWAITED in her sitting-room the return of the carriage.

It had been a great effort to let it go to the station without her. In fact she had ordered it to the front door, and put on her hat and coat in readiness.

But at the last minute it had seemed impossible to meet Ronnie on a railway platform.

So she sent the brougham off without her, went upstairs, put on a soft trailing gown specially admired by Ronnie, paused at the nursery to make sure all was quiet and ready, then came down to her sitting-room, and tried to listen for a sound other than the beating of her own heart.

The room looked very home-like and cosy. A fire crackled gaily on the hearth. The winter curtains were drawn; the orange lamp-shades cast a soft golden light around.

The tea-table stood ready—cups and plates for two. The firelight shone on the embossed brightness of the urn and teapot.

Ronnie's favourite low chair was ready for him.

The room seemed in every detail to whisper, "Home"; and the woman who waited knew that the home within her heart, yearning to receive and welcome and hold him close, after his long, long absence from her, was more tender, more beautiful, more radiant, than outward surroundings could possibly be made.

No word save the one telegram had come from Ronnie since her letter to Leipzig. But she knew he had been desperately busy; and, with the home-coming so near, letters would have seemed to him almost impossible.

He could not know how her woman's heart had yearned to have him say at once: "I am glad, and you did right."

Her nervousness increased, as the hour for the return of the carriage drew near.

She wished she could be sure of having time to run up again to the nursery with final instructions to nurse. Supposing baby woke, just as the carriage arrived, and the first sound Ronnie heard was the hungry wailing of his little son!

Passing into the hall, she stood listening at the foot of the stairs.

All was quiet on the upper landing.

She returned to the sitting-room, and rang the bell.

"Simpkins," she said to her butler, "listen for the carriage and be at the door when it draws up. It may arrive at any moment now. Tell Mr. West I am in here."

6

She sat down, determined to wait calmly; took up the paper and tried to read an article on foreign policy, It was then she discovered that her hands were trembling.

She laughed at herself and felt better.

"Oh, what will Ronnie think of me! That I, of all people, should unexpectedly become nervous!"

She walked over to the fireplace and saw reflected in the mirror over the mantelpiece, a very lovely, but a very white, face. She did not notice the loveliness, but she marked the pallor. It was not reassuring.

She tried to put another log on to the fire, but failed to grip it firmly with the little brass tongs, and it fell upon the rug. At that moment she heard the sharp trot of the horses coming up the last sweep of the park drive.

She flung the log on to the fire with her fingers, flew to the door and set it open; then returned to the table and stood leaning against it, her hands behind her, gripping the edge, her eyes upon the doorway. Ronnie would have to walk the whole length of the room to reach her. Thus she would see him—see the love in his eyes—before her own were hidden.

She heard Simpkins cross the hall and open the door.

The next moment the horses' hoofs pounded up the drive, and she heard the crunch of the wheels coming to a standstill on the wet gravel.

A murmur from Simpkins, then Ronnie's gay, joyous voice, as he entered the house.

"In the sitting-room? Oh, thanks! Yes, take my coat. No, not this. I will put it down myself."

Then his footsteps crossing the hall.

Then—Ronnie filled the doorway; tall, bronzed, radiant as ever! She had forgotten how beautiful he was. And—yes—the love in his eyes was just as she had known it would be—eager, glowing.

She never knew how he reached her; but she let go the

table and held out her arms. In a moment he was in them, and his were flung around her. His lips sought hers, but her face was hidden on his breast. She felt his kisses in her hair.

"Oh, Helen!" he said. "Helen! Why did I ever go!"

She held him closer still, sobbing a little.

"Darling, we both thought it right you should go. And —you didn't know."

"No," he agreed rather vaguely, "of course I didn't know." He thought she meant that he had not known how long the parting would seem, how insistent would be the need of each other. "I should not have gone, if I had known," he added, tenderly.

"I knew you wouldn't, Ronnie. But—I was all right."

"Of course you were all right. You know, you said we were a healthy couple, so I suppose there was no need to worry or to expect anything else. Was there? All the same I *did* worry—sometimes."

She waited for more.

It did not come. Ronnie was kissing her hair again.

"Were you glad when you had my letter, Ronnie?" she asked, very low.

"Which letter, sweet? I was always glad of every letter."

"Why, the last—the one to Leipzig."

"Oh, of course! Yes, I was very glad. I read it in your cousin's flat. I had just been showing him—oh, Helen! That reminds me—darling, I have something to show you! Such a jolly treasure—such a surprise! I left it in the hall. Would you like me to fetch it?"

He loosed his arms and she withdrew from them, looking up into his glowing face.

"Yes, Ronnie," she said. "Why, certainly. Do fetch it."

He rushed off into the hall. He fumbled eagerly with the buckles of the canvas bag. It had never taken so long, to draw the precious Infant forth.

He held it up to the hall lights. He wanted to make sure

that it was really as brown and as beautiful as it had always seemed to him.

Yes, it was as richly brown as the darkest horse-chestnut you ever saw in a bursting bur!

He walked back into the sitting-room, carrying it proudly before him.

Helen had just lighted the spirit-lamp beneath the swinging kettle on the brass stand. Her face was rather white again.

"Here it is, Helen," he said. "The most beautiful 'cello you ever saw! It is one hundred and fifty years old. It was made at Prague. I paid a hundred and fifty pounds for it."

Helen looked,

"That was a good deal to pay for a 'cello," she said, yet conscious as she spoke that—even as Peter on the Mount— she had made the remark chiefly because she "wist not what to say."

"Not a bit!" said Ronnie. "A chap in the orchestra at The Hague, with a fine 'cello of his own, told me he had never in his life handled such a beauty. He considered it a wonderful bargain."

"It *is* a beauty," said Helen, pouring hot water from the urn into the teapot, with a hand which trembled.

Ronnie wheeled a third chair up to the low tea-table, opposite his own particular seat, leaned his 'cello up against it, sat down, put his elbows on his knees, and glowed at it with enthusiasm.

"I knew you would say so, darling. Ever since I bought it, after choosing your organ at Zimmermann's, I have been thinking of the moment when I should show it to you; though an even greater moment is coming for us soon, Helen."

"Yes, Ronnie."

"Look how the two silver strings shine in the firelight. I call it the Infant of Prague."

"Why the 'Infant'?"

"Because it is a hundred and fifty years old; and because you have to be so careful not to bump its head, when you carry it about."

Helen put her hand to her throat.

"I think it is a foolish name for a violoncello," she said, coldly.

"Not at all," explained Ronnie. "It seems to me more appropriate every day. My 'cello is the nicest infant that ever was; does what it's told, gives no trouble, and only speaks when it's spoken to!"

Helen bent over the kettle. It was boiling. She could hear the water bubbling; the lid began making little tentative leaps. Without lifting her eyes, she made the tea.

Ronnie talked on volubly. It was so perfect to be back in his own chair; to watch Helen making tea; and to have the Infant safely there to show her.

Helen did not seem quite so much interested or so enthusiastic as he had expected.

Suddenly he remembered Aubrey's joke.

Helen at that moment was handing him his cup of tea. He took it, touching her fingers with his own as he did so; a well-remembered little sign between them, because the first time it had dawned upon Helen that Ronnie loved her, and wanted her to know it, was on a certain occasion when he had managed to touch her fingers with his, as she handed him a cup of tea.

He did so now, smiling up at her. He was so happy, that things were becoming a little dream-like again; not a nightmare—that would be impossible with Helen so near—but an exquisite dream; a dream too perfectly beautiful to be true.

"Darling," he said, "I brought the Infant home in a canvas bag. We must have a proper case made for it. Aubrey said *you* would probably want to put it into a bassinet! I suppose he thought your mind would be likely to run on bassinets. But the Infant always reminds me of the darkest horse-chestnut you ever saw in a bursting bur; so I intend to have a case of polished rosewood made for it, lined with white velvet."

Helen laughed, wildly.

"I have not the smallest desire, Ronald, to put your 'cello into a bassinet!" she said.

It dawned upon Ronnie that Helen was not pleased.

"It was a silly joke of Aubrey's. I told him so. I said I should tell you *he* said it, not I. Let's talk of something else."

He turned his eyes resolutely from the 'cello, and told her of his manuscript, of the wonderful experiences of his travels, his complete success in finding the long grass thirteen feet high, and the weird, wild setting his plot needed.

Suddenly he became conscious that Helen was not listening. She sat gazing into the fire; her expression cold and unresponsive.

Ronnie's heart stood still. Never before had he seen that look on Helen's face. Were his nightmares following him home?

For the first time in his life he had a sense of inadequacy. Helen was not pleased with him. He was not being what she wanted.

He fell miserably silent.

Helen continued to gaze into the fire.

The Infant of Prague calmly reflected the golden lamp-light in the wonderful depths of its polished surface.

Suddenly an inspiration came to Ronnie. Brightness returned to his face.

He stood up.

"Darling," he said. "I told you that an even greater moment was coming for us."

She rose also, and faced him, expectant.

He put out his hand and lifted the Infant.

"Helen, let's go to the studio, where I first told you I felt sure I could play a 'cello. We will sit there in the firelight as we did on that last evening, seven months ago, and you shall hear me make the Infant sing, for the very first time."

Then the young motherhood in Helen, arose and took her by the throat.

"Ronald!" she said. "You are utterly, preposterously, altogether selfish! I am ashamed of you!"

They faced each other across the table.

Every emotion of which the human soul is capable, passed over Ronnie's countenance—perplexity, amazement, anger, fury; grief, horror, dismay.

She saw them come and go, and come again; then, finally, resolve into a look of indignant misery.

At last he spoke.

"If that is your opinion, Helen," he said, "it is a pity I ever returned from the African jungle. Out there I could have found a woman who would at least have given me a welcome home."

Then his face flamed into sudden fury. He seized the cup from which he had been drinking, and flung up his hand above his head. His upper lip curled back from his teeth, in an angry snarl.

Helen gazed at him, petrified with terror.

His eyes met hers, and he saw the horror in them. Instantly, the anger died out of his. He lowered his hand, carefully examined the pattern on the cup, then replaced it gently in the saucer.

"I beg your pardon," he said. "I ought not to have said that—about another woman. There is but *one* woman for me; and, welcome or no welcome, there is but one home."

Then he turned from her, slowly, deliberately, taking his 'cello with him. He left the room, without looking back. She heard him cross the hall, pause as if to pick up something there; then pass down the corridor leading to the studio.

Listening intently, she heard the door of the studio close; not with a bang—Ronnie had banged doors before now—

but with a quiet irrevocability which seemed to shut her out, completely and altogether.

Sinking into the chair in which she had awaited his coming with so much eagerness of anticipation, Helen broke into an uncontrollable paroxysm of weeping.

CHAPTER XII

A FRIEND IN DEED

PRECISELY HOW long she remained alone in her sitting-room, Helen never knew; but it cannot have been the long hours it seemed; seeing that Simpkins did not appear to fetch the tea-tray, nor did nurse send down any message from the nursery.

Helen had wept herself into the calm of exhaustion, and was trying to decide what her next move should be, when the hoot of a motor sounded in the park. In another moment she heard it panting at the door. Then the bell pealed.

With the unfailing instinct of her kind, to hide private grief and show a brave front to the world, Helen flew to the mirror, smoothed her tumbled hair, put away her damp handkerchief; and, standing calmly beside the mantelpiece, one foot on the fender, awaited her unexpected visitor.

She heard voices in the hall, then Simpkins opened the door and tried to make an announcement, but some unseen force from behind whirled him away, and a broad-shouldered young man in an ulster, travel-stained and dishevelled, appeared in his stead, shut the door upon Simpkins, and strode into the lamplight, his cloth cap still on the back of his head, his keen dark eyes searching Helen's face eagerly.

His cap came off before he spoke to her; but, with his thick, short-cropped hair standing on end, a bare head only added to the wildness of his appearance.

He stopped when he reached the tea-table.

"Where's Ronnie?" he said, and he spoke as if he had been running for many miles.

"My husband is in the studio," replied Helen, with gentle dignity.

"What's he doing?"

"I believe he is playing his 'cello."

"Oh, lor! That wretched Infant! Is he all right?"

"So far as I know."

"What time did he get here?"

"At half-past four."

The dishevelled young man glanced at the clock.

"Oh, lor!" he said again. "To think I've travelled night and day and raced down from town in a motor to get here first, and he beat me by an hour and a half! However, if he's all right, no harm's done."

He dropped into Ronnie's chair, and rumpled his hair still further with his hands.

"I must try to explain," he said.

Then he lifted a rather white, very grubby face to Helen's. His lips twitched.

"I'm dry," he said; and dropped his face into his hands.

Helen rang the bell.

"Bring whisky and soda at once," she ordered, the instant Simpkins appeared in the doorway.

Then she crossed over, and laid her hand lightly on her visitor's broad shoulder.

"Don't try to explain," she said kindly, "until you have had something. I am sure I know who you are. You appear in all sorts of cricket and football groups in Ronnie's dressing-room. You are Ronnie's special chum, Dick Cameron."

Dick did not lift his head. As a matter of fact, at that moment he could not. But, though his throat contracted, so that speech became impossible, in his heart he was saying: "What a woman! Lor, what a woman! Ninety-nine out of a hundred would have offered me tea—and tea that had stood an hour; and the hundredth would have sent for a policeman! But she jumps instantly to whisky and soda; and then walks across and makes me feel at home. Eh, well! We shall save old Ronnie between us."

She administered the whisky and soda when it appeared; sitting gently beside him, in exceeding friendliness.

The rugged honesty of the youth appealed to her. His very grimness seemed but an earnest of his steadfast purpose, and suited her present mood of utter disillusion with the artistic and the beautiful.

Dick's look of keen alertness, his sense of forceful vigour, soon returned to him.

He stood up, surveyed himself in the glass, then turned with a rueful smile to Helen.

"It was both kind and brave of you, Mrs. West," he said, "not to send for a policeman."

Helen laughed. "I think I know an honest man when I see him, Dr. Dick. You must let me use the name by which I have always heard of you. Now, can you explain more fully?"

"Certainly," said Dick, getting out of his ulster, and sitting down. "But I must begin by asking a few more questions. Did you get your cousin's letter yesterday morning? It was absolutely essential you should receive it before Ronnie reached home. I hoped you would act upon it at once."

Helen gazed at him, aghast.

"I did receive my cousin's letter," she said.

"Was it quite explicit, Mrs. West?"

"It was absolutely explicit."

"Ah! Then on that point I admit I have wronged him. But you must excuse me if I say that I am inclined to consider your cousin a liar and a scoundrel."

Helen's face was white and stern. "I am afraid I have long known him to be both, Dr. Dick."

"Then you will not wonder that when I found he was not keeping his word to me, and bringing Ronnie home, I dashed off in pursuit.'"

"Was there ever any question of his returning with my husband?"

It was Dick's turn to look perplexed.

"Of course there was. In fact, he gave me his word in the matter. I mistrusted him, however, and the more I thought it over, the more uneasy I grew. Yesterday morning, the day he was to have crossed with Ronnie, I called at his flat and found he was expected back there to-day. I should dearly have liked to wait and wring his neck on arrival, but naturally Ronnie's welfare came first. I could not catch the night boat at The Hague, but I dashed off via Brussels, crossed from Boulogne this morning, reached London forty minutes too late for the 3 o'clock train to Hollymead. There was no other until five, and that a slow one. So I taxied off to a man I know in town, who owns several cars, borrowed his fastest, and raced down here, forty miles an hour. Even then I got here too late. However, no harm has been done. But you will understand that prompt action was necessary. What on earth was your cousin's little game?"

"It is quite inexplicable to me." said Helen, slowly, "that you should have any knowledge of my cousin's letter. Also, you have obviously been prompt, but I have not the faintest idea why prompt action was necessary."

"Didn't your cousin give you my message?"

"Your name was not mentioned in his letter."

"Did he tell you of Ronnie's critical condition?"

"He said Ronnie told him he had never felt fitter in his life, and added that he looked it."

Dick leapt to his feet, walked over to the window, and muffled a few remarks about Aubrey Treherne, in the curtains. Nevertheless Helen heard them.

"Is—Ronnie—ill?" she asked, with trembling lips.

Dick came back.

"Ronnie is desperately ill, Mrs. West. But, now he is safely at home, within easy reach of the best advice, we will soon have him all right again. Don't you worry."

But "worry" scarcely expressed Helen's face of agonised dismay.

"Tell me—all," she said.

Dick sat down and told her quite clearly and simply the text of his message to her through Aubrey, explaining and amplifying it with full medical details.

"Any violent emotion, either of joy, grief or anger, would probably have disastrous results. He apparently came to blows with your cousin during the evening he spent at Leipzig. Ronnie gave him a lovely thing in the way of lips. One recalls it now with exceeding satisfaction. When I saw your cousin afterwards he appeared to have condoned it. But it may account for his subsequent behaviour. Fortunately this sort of thing——" Dick glanced about him appreciatively—"looks peaceful enough."

Helen sat in stricken silence.

"It augurs well that he was able to stand the pleasure of his home-coming," continued Dr. Dick. "He must be extraordinarily better, if you noticed nothing unusual. Possibly he slept during the night-crossing. Also, I gave him some stuff to take on the way back, intended to clear his brain and calm him generally. Did he seem to you quite normal?"

Then Helen rose and stood before him with clasped hands.

"He seemed to me quite normal," she said, "because I had no idea of anything else. But now that I know the truth, of course I realise at once that he was not so. And, oh, Dr. Dick, I had a terrible scene with Ronnie!"

Dick stood up.

"Tell me," he said.

"I told Ronnie that he was utterly, preposterously, and altogether selfish, and that I was ashamed of him."

"Whew! You certainly did not mince matters," said Dr. Dick. "What had poor old Ronnie done?"

"He had talked, from the moment of his return, of very little save the 'cello he has brought home. He had suggested that it might amuse me to put it into a bassinet. Then when at last tea was over, he proposed, as the most delightful proceeding possible, that we should adjourn to the studio, and that I should sit and listen while he made a first attempt to play his 'cello—which, by, the way, he calls the 'Infant of Prague,' explaining to me that it is the nicest infant that ever was."

"Oh, that confounded Infant!" exclaimed Dr. Dick. "I have hated it from the first! But really, Mrs. West," he looked puzzled. "All this was no doubt enthusiasm misplaced. But then Ronnie always is a perfect infant himself, where new toys are concerned. You can hardly realise how much he has looked forward to showing you that 'cello. His behaviour also proved a decided tendency to self-absorption; but there the artistic temperament comes in, which always creates a world of its own in which it dwells content, often at the expense of duties and obligations connected with outer surroundings. We all know that this is Ronnie's principal failing. But—excuse me for saying so— it hardly deserved quite so severe an indictment from you."

Helen wrung her hands.

Suddenly Dr. Dick took them both, firmly in his.

"Why don't you tell me the truth?" he said.

Then Helen told him.

She never could remember afterwards exactly how she told him, and no one but Helen ever knew what Dr. Dick said and did. But, months later—when in her presence aspersions were being cast on Dick for his indomitable ambition, his ruthless annihilation of all who stood in his way, his utter lack of religious principle and orthodox belief—Helen, her sweet face shadowed by momentary sadness, her eyes full of pathetic remembrance, spoke up for Ronnie's chum. "He may be a bad old thing in many ways," she said; "I admit that the language he uses is calculated to make his great-aunt Louisa, of sacred memory, turn in her gravel But—he is a tower of strength in one's hour of need."

   .   .   .   .

"No," said Dick, after a while, gazing straight before him into the fire, his chin in his hands; "I can't believe Ronnie knew it. He was just in the condition to become frantically excited by such news. He would have been desperately anxious about you; wild that you should have gone through it alone, and altogether absorbed in the idea of coming home and seeing his child. The Infant of Prague would have had its shining nose put completely out of joint. I don't believe Ronnie ever had your letter. Write to the *Poste Restante* at Leipzig, and you will receive it back."

"Impossible," said Helen. "He opened and read it that evening in Aubrey's flat. He told Aubrey the news, and Aubrey mentioned it in his letter to me."

Dick looked grave.

"Well then," he said. "old Ronnie is in an even worse case than I feared. I think we should go at once and look him up. I told my friend's chauffeur to wait; so, if further advice is needed to-night, we can send the car straight back to town with a message. Where is Ronnie?"

"He took his 'cello, and went off to the studio. I heard him shut the door."

"Show me the way," said Dr. Dick.

With his hand on the handle of the sitting-room door, he paused.

"I suppose you—er—feel quite able to forgive poor old Ronnie, now?" he asked.

The yearning anguish in Helen's eyes made answer enough.

They crossed the hall together; but—as they passed down the corridor leading to the studio—they stopped simultaneously, and their eyes sought one another in silent surprise and uncertainty.

The deep full tones of a 'cello, reached them where they stood; tones so rich, so plaintively sweet, so full of passion and melody, that, to the anxious listeners in the dimly lighted corridor, they gave the sense of something weird, something altogether uncanny in its power, unearthly in its beauty.

They each spoke at the same moment.

"It cannot be Ronnie," they said.

"It must be Ronnie," amended Helen. "There is no one else in the house."

"*You* go in," whispered Dick. "I will wait here. Call, if you want me. Don't startle him. Go in very softly. Be very—er—*you* know?"

Helen moved forward alone.

She laid her hand upon the handle of the studio door.

She wished the weird music within would cease for one moment, that she might feel more able to enter.

Cold shivers ran down her spine.

Try as she would, she could not connect that music with Ronnie.

Somebody else was also in the studio, of that she felt quite certain.

She nearly went back to Dick.

Then—rating herself for cowardice—she turned the handle of the door and passed in.

Dick saw her disappear.

Almost at that moment, the 'cello-playing ceased; there was a crash, a cry from Helen, a silence, and then—a wild shriek from Helen, a sound holding so much of fear and of horror, that Dick shouted in reply as he dashed forward.

He found himself in a low room, oak-panelled, lighted only by the uncertain flame of a log-fire. The door by which Dick had entered was to the left of the fireplace. On the wall at the farther end of the room, opposite both door and fireplace, hung an immense mirror in a massive gilt frame.

On the floor in the centre of the room lay Ronnie, unconscious, on his back. The chair upon which he had been sitting and which had gone over backwards with him, lay broken beneath him. His 'cello rested on his chest. He gripped it there, with both his hands. They fell away from it, as Dick looked at him.

Ronnie's wife knelt on the floor beside him, but she was not looking at Ronnie. She was staring, with white face and starting eyes, into the mirror. Her left arm, stretched out before her, was rigid with horror, from the shoulder to the tip of the pointing finger.

"Look, Dick!" she shrieked. "Oh, heavens! Look!"

Dick flashed up the electric light; then looked into the mirror.

He saw himself loom large; dishevelled, grimy, travel-stained. Then he saw Ronnie and the Infant in a dark heap on the floor, and the white face of Ronnie's wife, kneeling beside him with outstretched arm and eyes upon the mirror. On the other side of Ronnie, in the very centre of the scene, stood a queer old chair of Italian workmanship, the heads of lions completing its curved arms, on its carved back the *fleur-de-lis* of Florence, its seat of padded leather, embossed in crimson and gold.

This was all Dick saw, excepting the leaping flames of the fire beyond.

And even as he looked, Helen's arm fell to her side; he saw her turn, lift the Infant off Ronnie's breast; and, bending over him, draw his head on to her lap.

Dick turned from the mirror. The scene in the room was identical with the reflection, in all points save one.

The Florentine chair was under Ronnie. It had fallen with him. Its back was broken. Not until he had lifted his friend from the floor did Dr. Dick see the panelled *fleur-de-lis* of Florence, nor the crimson and gold of the embossed leather seat.

As he and Helen together loosed Ronnie's collar and tie, she whispered: "Did—*you*—see?"

"This is no time for staring into mirrors," said Dr. Dick, crossly. "I saw that *I* need a good wash; and *you*, some sal volatile? But we shall have plenty to do for Ronnie before we can find leisure to think of ourselves. Send a couple of men here; sturdy fellows whom you can trust. Order that car to the door; then bring me a pencil, a sheet of note-paper and an envelope. There is just one man in the world who can help us now, and we must have him here with as little delay as possible."

When Helen had left the room, Dick glanced furtively over his shoulder into the mirror.

The Italian chair, in the reflection, now lay broken on the floor!

"Hum!" said Dr. Dick. "Not bad, that—for an Infant! Precocious, I call it. We must have that 'cello re-christened, the '*Demon* of Prague'!"

CHAPTER XIII

RONNIE FACES THE UPAS

RONNIE HAD walked from his wife's sitting-room, along the corridor and into the studio, in a state of stunned stupefaction.

He carried his 'cello in one hand, its case and bow, which he had picked up in the hall, in the other; but he had for the moment completely forgotten the Infant.

He leaned it against a chair, laid down the case, closed the studio door; then walked to the fireplace.

He stood looking at the great crackling logs, and into the glowing heart of the fire beneath them.

"Utterly, preposterously, altogether selfish," he repeated slowly. "That is what my wife considers me; that is as I appear to Helen. Utterly—preposterously—altogether—selfish. She is so lovely—she is so perfect! I—I have longed for her so! But I am utterly, preposterously, altogether selfish!"

He put his arms upon the mantelpiece and dropped his head upon them. He felt a queer contraction in his throat, a stinging beneath his eyelids, such as he had not experienced since the days of childish mortifications and sorrows. But the instinctive manliness of him, held back the actual tears. He was debarred, even in solitude, from that form of relief.

Presently he lifted his head, took out his pocket-book, and wrote down the words, spelling each with a capital letter.

He looked long at them; then suddenly exclaimed: "U, P, A, S! Why, it is the Upas tree; the deadly, mysterious, poisonous Upas tree! I found it in the jungle. I felt ill the night I camped beneath it. I have never felt quite well since. The nightmares began on that night; and the nightmares have followed me home. This is the worst of all. Helen calls me the Upas tree—the poisoner of her content. Utterly, preposterously, altogether selfish!"

He turned on the electric lights, and walked up and down the room, with desperate, restless tread.

"Poisoning all it touches," he said. "Blasting the life of all who pass beneath its deadly foliage—U, P, A, S—Upas."

He paused before the great mirror, gazing at his own reflection.

He put his face quite close to the glass, staring into his burning eyes.

Then he struck at the reflection with his clenched fist. "Upas tree!" he snarled. "Take that, and be damned!"

He had hurt his knuckles. He walked back to the fire, rubbing them carefully with his left hand.

"Poor old chap," he said. "It *is* hard lines! You meant well; but all the while you were a Upas tree. '*I, Helen, take thee, Upas, to be my wedded husband.*' Poor lovely Helen! What a bargain!"

He sat down in a deep basket-chair, lighted a cigarette, pushed another chair into position, exactly in front of him, with his foot; then filling it, one by one, with friends of his own and Helen's, held conversation with them.

"Quite right, my dear Mrs. Dalmain! You need not now confine yourself to *looking* your disapproval; you can *say* exactly what you think. You see, Helen herself has told me the worst truth of all. I am a Upas tree. She sums me up thus: U, P, A, S! You can hardly beat that, Mrs. Dalmain. In fact, you look distressed. I can see that your kind heart is sorry for me. Helen said you were a wonderful person to turn to in trouble. There is no one in the world quite like you. Well, now's your chance to prove it; for surely nobody ever came to you in more desperate trouble. If you wish to be really kind and comforting, talk to me of my wife. Say how sweet, and lovely she is. Say that her arms are tender, her eyes gentle and kind. I am the thirsty traveller in the desert, who sights pure water, hastens eagerly forward, and finds—a mirage! But a deadly stream flows from the roots of the Upas—Hullo! Here comes Aubrey Treherne. Look out, Mrs. Dalmain! He owes you a grudge. Hey, presto! vanish from the chair, or Helen's cousin will lean over, with a bleeding face, threatening to kill you with both hands! . . .

"Good evening, Cousin Aubrey. How is your lip to-night? You mustn't kiss Helen again, until that lip is well. Helen will be ashamed of you for not being able to put fuel into a stove without knocking your lip. Fie, man! Poor, happy Ronnie, going home to show his wife his 'cello, believed you. But the Upas tree knows! You can't deceive the Upas tree, you liar! You may as well tell Helen that you wounded your lip on a branch of her Upas tree. . . .

"Hullo, Dick! Come in, and welcome! Sit down, old boy. I want to ask you something. Hist! Listen! That motor, which hooted in the park a moment ago, contained a policeman—so it is essential we should know whether there is any by-law in Leipzig against men, as trees, walking. Because you weren't walking about with a man, you know, but with a Upas tree. When in doubt, ask—my wife! It would have made a sensational paragraph in the papers: 'Arrest of a Upas tree, in the streets of Leipzig!' Worse than 'Arrest of the Infant of Prague.' . . . Why! Where is the Infant?"

He turned and saw his 'cello, where he had placed it, leaning against a chair.

He rose, took it up, and walked over to the piano.

"A, D, G, C. 'Allowable delights grow commonplace!' What did the fiend mean? C, G, D, A. 'Courage gains desired aims.' That's better! We aimed pretty straight at his lying mouth."

He opened the piano, struck the notes, and tuned the 'cello exactly as he had seen Aubrey do.

At the first sound of the strings his mood changed. All bitterness passed out of his face. A look of youth and hope dawned in it.

He carried the 'cello back to the circle of chairs. He placed it where it had stood before; then lay back in his own seat smiling dreamily at the empty chair opposite.

"Helen," he said, "Darling, I don't really play the piano, I only strum. But there is one instrument, above all others, which I have always longed to play. I have it now. I own the 'cello I have always loved and longed for; the 'cello on which I used to play a hundred years ago. Now I am going to play to you; and you will forget everything in this world, my wife, excepting that I love you."

He drew the Infant between his knees; then realised at once that his chair was too low.

Rising, he went over to a corner where, against the wall, stood a beautiful old chair which he and Helen had brought back, the winter before, from Italy. Its arms and feet of walnut wood, were carved into lions' heads and paws. Its back bore, in a medallion, the Florentine *fleur-de-lis*. The high padded seat was of embossed gold, on crimson leather.

Ronnie placed this queer old chair in the centre of the room, facing the great mirror.

Then he clicked off the electric lights, stirred the fire, and threw on a couple of fresh logs.

The flames shot up, illumining the room.

CHAPTER XIV

AS IN A MIRROR

RONNIE RETURNED to the Florentine chair, took the 'cello between his knees, placed his thumb behind its polished neck and his fingers on the ebony finger-board. He let them glide lightly up and down the strings, making no sound. Then he raised the bow in his right hand, and slowly, softly, sounded the four open notes.

Each tone was deep and true; there was no rasp—no uneven scraping of the bow.

The log-fire burned up brightly.

He waited. A great expectation filled him.

He was remembering something he had long forgotten.

Looking straight before him at his own reflection in the mirror, he smiled to see how correctly he held the 'cello. The Infant seemed at home between his knees.

The sight of himself and the Infant thus waiting together, gave him peculiar pleasure.

The fire burned low.

His reflected figure dimmed and faded. A misty shadow hid it from his eyes. He could just see the shining of the silver strings, and the white line of his linen cuff.

Then suddenly, he forgot all else save that which he had been trying to remember.

He felt a strong tremor in his left wrist. He was gripping the neck of the 'cello. The strings were biting deep into the flesh of his finger-tips.

He raised the bow and swept it across the strings.

Low throbbing music filled the studio, and a great delight flooded Ronnie's soul.

He dared not give conscious thought to that which he was doing; he could only go on doing it.

He knew that he—he himself—was at last playing his own 'cello. Yet it seemed to him that he was merely listening, while another played.

Two logs fell together in the fire behind him.

Bright flames shot up, illumining the room.

Ronnie raised his eyes and looked into the mirror.

He saw therein reflected, the 'cello and the Italian chair; but the figure of a man sat playing, and that man was not himself; that figure was not his own.

A grave, white face, set off by straight black hair, a heavy lock of which fell over the low forehead; long white fingers gliding up and down the strings, lace ruffles falling from the wrists. The knees, gripping the 'cello, were clad in black satin breeches, black silk stockings were on the shapely legs; while on the feet, planted firmly upon the floor, gleamed diamond shoe-buckles.

Ronnie gazed at this reflection.

Each movement of the gliding bow, corresponded to the rhythm of the music now throbbing through the studio.

Ronnie played on, gazing into the mirror. The man in

the mirror did not lift his eyes, nor look at Ronnie. Either they were bent upon the 'cello, or he played with them fast closed.

Ronnie dared not look down at his own hands. He could feel his fingers moving up and down the strings, as moved the fingers in the mirror. He feared he should see lace ruffles falling from his wrists, if he looked at his own hands.

The fire burned low again.

Still Ronnie played on, staring before him as he played. The music gained in volume and in beauty.

The fire burned lower. The room was nearly dark. The reflection was almost hidden.

Ronnie, straining his eyes, could see only the white line of the low square forehead.

He wished the eyes would lift and look at him, piercing the darkness of the darkening room.

Another log fell. Again flames darted upwards. Each detail in the mirror was clear once more.

The playing grew more rapid. Ronnie felt his fingers flying, yet pressing deeply as they flew.

The right foot of the figure, placed farther back than the left, was slightly raised. The heel was off the floor.

Ronnie's right heel was also lifted.

Then, looking past the figure in the chair, he marked behind him, where in the reflection of the studio should have been the door, heavy black curtains hanging in sombre folds. And, even as Ronnie noticed these, they parted; and the lovely face of a woman looked in.

As Ronnie saw that face he remembered many things— things of exquisite joy, things of poignant sorrow; things inexpressible except in music, unutterable except in tone.

The 'cello sobbed, and wailed, and sang itself slowly into a minor theme; yet the passion of the minor was more subtle, sweeter far, than the triumph of the major.

The woman glided in.

Ronnie watched her. She came and softly stood behind the Florentine chair.

Apparently she made no sound. The 'cellist did not raise his eyes. He appeared totally unconscious of her presence.

The woman bent her beautiful head, observing him closely. Following her eyes, Ronnie saw a ruffle of old lace falling from the 'cellist's throat, a broad crimson ribbon crossing his breast, on which glittered a diamond star.

The woman waited.

Ronnie watched.

The 'cellist played on.

The fire burned low.

Then another log fell. Again flames darted upward.

Ronnie saw the woman lay her left hand noiselessly upon the back of the Italian chair, then slip her right behind her and take something bright, off a table covered with bright things. And, as he watched, she flung her right hand high above her head, and in it, point downwards, gleamed the sharp blade of a dagger.

Her eyes met Ronnie's in the mirror. A gleam of malicious triumph shot from them.

He knew she was about to kill the unconscious 'cellist.

His one thought was to warn and to save him. He knew no sound he made could be heard in a past century; but whatever he himself now did, he instinctively felt the 'cellist in the mirror would also do.

With a desperate effort he stopped the movement of the bow.

He had just time to see the 'cellist in the mirror also pause.

Then Ronnie dropped his bow, gripped the 'cello with both hands, and, as the swift blow fell, drew the body of the 'cello up over his breast.

Then the back of his chair seemed to give way; his feet left the floor, and he fell over backwards—down—down—down—into a never ending abyss of throbbing, palpitating, rolling blackness.

PART IV

CHAPTER XV

THE FOG LIFTS

WHEN RONNIE came to himself, emerging quite suddenly from a long, confused dream, which had held many voices, many happenings over which he had exercised no control and which were too indefinite to be remembered, he found himself sitting on a seat, on the esplanade at Hazelbeach.

A crisp, wintry feeling was in the air; but the sun was brilliant, and the high ground behind, sheltered the sea-front from wind.

He was muffled in his fur coat, and felt quite warm.

The first thing he consciously noticed was the sparkling of the ripple on the calm water.

There is something particularly reviving and inspiriting about sunshine on the gaily moving sea. The effect is produced with so little apparent effort. The sun just shines; the water just moves; and lo, hosts of sparkling diamonds!

Ronnie watched it in silence for some time, before giving any sign that he actually saw it.

He was anxious carefully to take his bearings, without appearing to do so.

Helen sat beside him on the seat. She kept up a flow of conversation, in the kind, cheerful, intelligent voice in which you talk to a child who has to be kept happy and amused.

Ronnie let her go on talking in that voice, while he took his bearings.

He glanced at her, furtively, once; then turned his eyes seaward again.

Helen, also, was wearing a fur coat, and a pretty grey fur toque on her soft hair. Her face seemed thinner than it used to be; but the sea breeze and sunshine had brought a bright colour to her cheeks.

Ronnie's eyes left the ripples, and wandered cautiously up and down the shore.

The beach was deserted. No moving figures dotted the esplanade. Helen and he would have been alone, had it not been for one tiresome man who sat reading on the next seat to theirs. He looked like a superior valet or upper footman, in a bowler and a black morning coat. He was just out of earshot; but his presence prevented Ronnie from feeling himself alone with Helen, and increased the careful caution with which he took his bearings.

At last he felt the moment had arrived to stop Helen's well-meant attempts at amusing him.

The man on the other seat was a dozen yards off to the right. Helen sat quite close to him on the left. He turned his back on the other seat and looked earnestly into his wife's face.

"Helen," he said, quietly, "how did we get here?"

"We motored, darling. It isn't very far across country, though to get here by train we should have to go up to town and down again."

"When did we come?"

"Yesterday. Ronnie, do look at those funny little wooden houses just beyond us on the esplanade. They take the place of bathing-machines, or bathing-tents, in summer. They can be hired just for the morning, or you can engage one for the whole time of your visit, and furnish it comfortably. Don't you think it is quite a good idea? And people give them such grand names. I saw one called 'Woodstock,' and another 'Highcombe House.' If we took one, we should have to call it 'The Grange.' "

"Helen, you have told me all about those little huts

twice already, during the last half-hour. Only, last time you had seen one called 'Runnymead,' and another called 'The Limes.' Presently, if you like, we will walk along and read all the names. It is just the kind of thing which would appeal to our joint sense of humour. But first you must answer a few more questions. Helen—where is my 'cello?"

"At home, Ronnie."

"Was it broken?"

Helen looked distressed. "No, darling, it was not injured at all. It is safely put away. Look how the sunlight sparkles on those distant ripples!"

"I have finished with the ripples, thank you, darling. Helen, I know I've been desperately ill. But I'm all right now, and I want you to tell me all about it."

He saw her glance past him, at the man who sat reading on the next seat.

"Don't worry about him," he said. "He can't overhear. If you think he can, let's move on."

"No, no!" said Helen, quickly. "We are so cosy here in the sunshine. Ronnie, do you see those——"

"No, dear," he said, "I don't! At this moment I see nothing but you. And I decline to have my attention drawn any more to the exciting things to be seen on the shore at Hazelbeach in winter. . . . Oh, yes, I knew it was Hazelbeach! Five years ago I spent a jolly week here with some friends. We hired a little wooden hut and called it 'Buckingham Palace,' I remember."

He slipped his hand into her muff, capturing both hers.

Her look of anxiety and alarm went to his heart. He had never seen Helen frightened before; and he knew with unerring instinct that she was afraid—*of him*.

It was hard; for he was desperately tired in mind and body. To subside into passive acquiescence and watch the ripples again, would be the easier way. But he must make a fight for his newly-recovered sanity and reason, and to convince Helen in the matter seemed the first thing to be accomplished.

Her hands were shaking in her muff. He held them firmly with his.

"Darling," he said, "I know I have been very bad. I was ill in Leipzig, though I didn't know it. But Dick Cameron told me I ought not to have been going about there. I suppose since then I have been quite off my head. But, oh, Helen, can't you see—can't you *see*, darling—that I am all right again now? I can remember practically nothing which has happened since I played my 'cello in front of the mirror in the studio. But, up to that moment, I remember everything quite clearly; my travels, my manuscript, the time when I began to get feverish and lost my sleep—I can see now the very spot where I camped when I had my first nightmare. Then working night and day on board ship, then Leipzig, The Hague, London in a fog; then home—to you. Helen, it has all come back. Can't you realise that the clouds have lifted; can't you believe, my own dear girl, that my mind is clear again? Look at the sunshine on the sea, dispelling the morning mists. *In hoc signo vinces!* You said the path of clear shining was the way to victory. Well, I have conquered whatever it was which poisoned my brain for a while. I am absolutely myself again now. Can't you believe it, Helen?"

The tears were running down her cheeks. She looked full into his earnest eyes.

"Oh, Ronnie, you do look different! You do look your own dear self. Oh, Ronnie, my own! But Dick is coming back to-morrow. He went up to town only this morning. He will tell us what to do. Till then, don't you think we had better just talk about the sea, and the little houses, and —and how happy we are?"

"No, Helen," he said firmly. "We are not happy yet.

I must know more. How long is it since that evening in the studio?"

"About a month, darling. This is Christmas week. To-morrow will be Christmas Eve."

Ronnie considered this in silence.

Then: "Let's walk up and down," he said. "It ought to be too cold to sit about in Christmas week."

She rose and they walked along the sea-front together.

Ronnie glanced behind them. The man on the seat had risen also and was following at a little distance.

"What cheek of that chap," he said. "He seems determined to overhear our conversation. Shall I tell him to be off?"

"No, dear; please don't," she answered hurriedly. "He cannot possibly overhear us."

Presently she dropped her muff and stooped to pick it up. But Ronnie turned also, and saw her make a sign to the man following them, who at once sat down on the nearest seat.

Then poor Ronnie knew.

"I suppose he is a keeper," he said.

"Oh, no, darling! He is only a trained attendant: just a sort of valet for you. Such a nice man and so attentive. He brushes your clothes."

"I see," said Ronnie. "Valets are quite useful people. But they do not as a rule sit reading in the middle of the morning, on the next seat to their master and mistress! Do they? However, if Dick is coming to-morrow, we can discuss the valet question with him. Take my arm, Helen. I feel a bit shaky when I walk. Now tell me—why did we come here?"

"They thought the change of scene, the perfect quiet, and the bracing air might do wonders for you, Ronnie."

"Who were 'they'?"

"Dr. Dick and—a friend of his."

"I see. Well, I won't bully you into telling me things you are afraid I ought not to know. But I will tell you just how much I *do* know. It is all a queer sort of black dream. I absolutely can't remember *seeing* anything, until I found myself watching the sparkle of the ripples on the sea. But I vaguely remember *hearing* things. There was always a kind voice. Of course that was yours, Helen. Also there was a kind hand. I used to try not to do anything which could hurt the kind hand. Then, there were several strange voices; they came and went. Then there was Mrs. Dalmain. When her voice was there I always tried to do at once what the strange voices and the kind voice wished; because I was horribly afraid of being left alone with Mrs. Dalmain! Then I sometimes thought I heard a baby cry. Wasn't that queer?"

Helen did not answer. A deep flush overspread her face, mounting from her chin to the roots of her hair. Was Ronnie going to remember?

"The kind voice used to say: 'Take him away, Nurse'; but I am vague about this; because I was miles down a deep well when it happened, and the baby was up at the top. I expect I got the idea from having called my 'cello the Infant of Prague. Did you hear me playing, on that evening, Helen?"

"Yes, I heard."

"Was it beautiful?"

"Very beautiful, Ronnie."

"I am longing to get back to play my 'cello again."

"By and by, dear."

"Did I talk much of the 'cello when I was ill?"

"A good deal. But you talked chiefly of your travels and adventures; such weird things, that the doctors often thought they were a part of your delirium. But I found them all clearly explained in your manuscript. I hope you won't mind, Ronnie. They asked me to glance through it, in order to see whether anything to be found there threw light on your illness. But of course you know, dearest, I could not do that. I never 'glanced through' any manuscript of yours yet. Either I do not touch them at all, or I read them carefully every word. I read this carefully."

"Is it all right?"

"Ronnie, it is magnificent! Quite the best thing you have done yet. Such brilliant descriptive writing. Even in the midst of my terrible anxiety, I used to be carried right away from all my surroundings. Of course I do not yet know the end; but when you are able to work again we can talk it all over, and you will tell me."

His sad face brightened. A look of real gladness came into it; the first she had seen for so long.

"I am glad it is all right," he said, simply. "I thought it was. I am glad I am not altogether a rotter."

After that they walked on in silence. His last remark had been so unexpected in its bitterness, that Helen could find no words in which to answer it.

She glanced at her watch. It was almost time for luncheon. She pointed out their hotel.

"Come, darling; we can talk more easily indoors. We have a charming private sitting-room, overlooking the sea."

He turned at once; but as they entered the hotel gardens he said suddenly: "Did I talk of a Upas tree, while I was off my head?"

"Yes, Ronnie, constantly. In fact you thought you *were* a Upas tree!"

"I *knew* I was a Upas tree," said Ronnie.

"Why?"

"Because my wife told me so, the evening I came home. How do you spell 'Upas'?"

"U, P, A, S. Oh, Ronnie, what do you mean?"

He paused, and shading his eyes, looked away over the sunny sea to where the vessels, from the Hook of Holland, come into port.

"Just that," he said. "Exactly that. Utterly, preposterously, altogether selfish. That is the Upas tree."

"Oh, Ronnie," she cried, "if you knew——"

But Ronnie had seen a bowler hat behind the hedge. He called its wearer forward.

"Mrs. West tells me you are my valet," he said. "Kindly show me to my room."

CHAPTER XVI

"HE *MUST* REMEMBER"

DICK ARRIVED very early the next morning, having to be off again by the twelve o'clock train, in order to reach that evening the place where he was due to spend Christmas.

A telegram from Helen had prepared him for a change in Ronnie, but hardly for the complete restoration of mental balance which he saw in his friend, as they hailed one another at the railway station.

Ronnie had breakfasted early, in order to meet Dick's train. He had said nothing of his plan to Helen, merely arranging his breakfast-hour overnight with the "valet."

He walked to the station alone; but, arrived there, found the "valet" on the platform.

"Thought I might be wanted, sir, to carry the doctor's bag," he explained, touching his hat. But, just as the train rounded the bend, he remarked: "Better stand back a little, sir," and took Ronnie firmly by the arm.

Ronnie could have knocked him down; but realised that this would be the surest way to find himself more than ever hedged in by precautions. So he stood back, in wrathful silence, and, as Dick's gay face appeared at the window of a third-class smoker, the "valet" loosed his hold and disappeared. It may here be recorded that this was the last time Ronnie saw him. Apparently he found it necessary to carry Mr. Dick's bag all the way back to town.

"Hullo, old chap!" cried Dick.

"Hullo, Dick!" said Ronnie. "This is better than Leipzig, old man. I'm all right. I must give you a new thermometer!"

"You shall," said Dick. "After Christmas we'll have a spree together in town and choose it. No need to tell me you're all right, Ronnie. It's writ large on you, my boy. He who runs may read!"

"Well, I wish you'd write it large on other people," said Ronnie, as they walked out of the station.

"What do you mean?"

"Dick, I'm having a devil of a time! There's a smug chap in a bowler hat who is supposed to be my valet. When I went to bed last night, I found I had a decent room enough opening out of the sitting-room. I was obviously expected to turn in there, asking no questions; so I turned in. But the valet person slept in a room communicating with mine. The latch and the lock of the door between, had been tampered with. The door wouldn't shut, so I had to sleep all night with that fellow able to look in upon me at any moment. After I had been in bed a little while, I remembered something I had left in the sitting-room and wanted. I got up quietly to fetch it. That door was locked, on the sitting-room side!"

"Poor old boy! We'll soon put all that right. You see you were pretty bad, while you *were* bad; and all kinds of precautions were necessary. We felt sure of a complete recovery, and I always predicted that it would be sudden. But it is bound to take a little while to get all your surroundings readjusted. Why not go home at once? Pack up and go back to Hollymead this afternoon, and have a real jolly Christmas there—you, and Helen, and the kid."

"The kid?" queried Ronnie perplexed. "What kid? Oh, you mean my 'cello—the Infant of Prague."

8

Dick, meanwhile, had bitten his tongue severely.

"Yes, the jolly old Infant of Prague, of course. Is it 'he,' 'she,' or 'it'? I forget."

"It," replied Ronnie, gravely. "In the peace of its presence one forgets all wearying 'he and she' problems. Yes, I want most awfully to get back to my 'cello. I want to make sure it is not broken; and I want to make sure it is no dream, that I can play. But—I don't want to go, unless I can go alone. Can't you prescribe complete solitude, as being absolutely essential for me? Dick, I'm wretched! I don't care where I go; but I want to get away by myself."

"Why, old man?"

"Because my wife still considers me insane."

"Nonsense, Ron! And don't talk of being insane. You were never that. Some subtle malarial poison, we shall never know what, got into your blood, affected your brain, and you've had a bad time—a very bad time—of being completely off your balance; the violent stage being followed by loss of memory, and for a time, though mercifully you knew nothing about it, complete loss of sight. But these things returned, one by one; and, as soon as you were ready for it, you awoke to consciousness, memory, and reason. There is no possible fear of the return of any of the symptoms, unless you come again in contact with the poison; hardly likely, as it attacked you in Central Africa. Of course, as I say, we shall never know precisely what the poison was."

Then Ronnie spoke, suddenly. "It was the Upas tree," he said. "I camped near it. My nightmares began that night. I never felt well, from that hour."

"Rubbish!" said Dr. Dick. "More likely a poisonous swamp. The Upas tree is a myth."

"Not at all," insisted Ronnie. "It is a horrid reality. I had seen the one in Kew Gardens. I recognised it directly, yet I camped in its shadow. Dick, do you know what the Upas stands for?"

"What?"

"Selfishness! It stands for any one who is utterly, preposterously, altogether selfish."

"Oh, buck up, old man!" cried Dick. "We are all selfish—every mother's son of us! Perhaps that's why! Most men's mothers spoil them, and their wives continue the process. But you will be selfish with a vengeance, if you don't buck up and give that splendid wife of yours a good time now. She has been through—such a lot. Ronnie, you will never quite realise—well, *I* never knew such a woman, excepting, perhaps, Mrs. Dalmain; and of course she has not your wife's beauty. I haven't the smallest intention of ever coming under the yoke myself. But I assure you, old chap, if you had pegged out, as you once or twice seemed likely to do, I should have had a jolly good try as to whether I couldn't chip in, by and by."

"Confound you!" said Ronnie. But he laughed, and felt better.

.   .   .   .   .   .

Dr. Dick saw Helen alone.

"Well," he said, "so we've pulled him through. Ronnie's all right now. No more need for watching and planning, and guarding; in fact, the less he realises the precautions which were necessary, the better. I shall take Truscott back to town with me. He seems to have done awfully well. I suppose you have no complaints. Why don't you hire a car and run straight back home with Ronnie this afternoon. Think what a jolly Christmas you might have. Show him the boy as a Christmas present! I believe he is keen to be at home; and the less you thwart him now, the better. Don't suggest it until I am gone; but send a wire home at once to say you are probably returning this afternoon. Then your people will make all needed preparations for the festive day; turkeys and holly, and all that sort

of thing; have fires lighted everywhere, and all in readiness.
My old sweetheart, Mrs. Blake, will put on cherry-coloured
ribbons, and black satin, and be in the hall to receive you!
You had better mention, in the wire, that I am not coming;
then she won't waste her time hanging mistletoe in likely
corners."

Helen wrote the telegram, rang, and gave it to a page.

Then she turned to Dr. Dick.

"Ronnie is *not* fully himself, yet," she said.

Dick looked at her keenly. "How so?"

"He professes to remember, and does remember, everything which happened, up to the final crash in the studio.
Yet he has made no mention to me of—of our child."

"He is shy about it," suggested Dick. "You speak first."

"I cannot," she replied. "It is for Ronald to do that."

"Ah, you dear women!" moralised the young bachelor.
"You remind me of Nebuchadnezzar—no, I mean Naaman.
You bravely ford the rushing waters of your Abanas and
your Pharpars, and then you buck-jump at the little river
Jordan!"

"My dear Dick, I am becoming accustomed to the extraordinary inaptness of your scriptural allusions. But this is
hardly a *small* matter between me and Ronnie. I am ready
to make every allowance for his illness and loss of memory;
but I don't see how I can start life with him at home, until
he manages to remember a thing of such vital import in
our wedded life. He may be sane on every other point.
I cannot consider him sane on this."

"Shall I tell him?" suggested Dick.

"No, let him remember. He can remember his Infant
of Prague; his mind is full of that again. Why should he not
be able to remember my baby son?"

"Oh, lor!" sighed Dr. Dick. "Why not put that poser
to Ronnie direct, instead of putting it to me? Forgive me
for saying so, but you are suffering just now from a reaction,

after the terrible strain through which you have passed. And Ronnie is wretched too, because he remembers how you let fly at him that evening, and he thinks you really meant it."

"I did," said Helen. "Of course, had I known how ill he was, poor old boy, I should have been more patient. But I have a little son to consider now, as well as Ronnie. I *did* think him selfish, and I *do*."

"My dear angel," said Dr. Dick, "we are all selfish, every mother's son of us; and it is you blessed women who make us so."

She looked at him, with softening eyes. "*You* are not selfish, Dick," she said.

"I am," he answered; "and a long chalk worse than Ronnie. I combine ambition with my selfishness. I jolly well mean to get to the top of the tree, and I don't care how I get there. I down every one who dares stand in my way; or—I use them as stepping-stones. There! Isn't that a worse Upas tree than poor old Ronnie's? Mine is a life untouched by love, or any gentler feelings. All that sort of thing was killed in me when I was quite a little chap. It is the story of a broken halo. Perhaps I'll tell it you some day. Meanwhile, this being Christmas Eve and not Ash Wednesday, I'll make no more confessions. Don't you want to hear the result of my psychic investigations, concerning our mirror experiences?"

"Exceedingly," said Helen. "Have you time to tell me now?"

"Heaps of time. It won't take long. Last night I told the whole story to a man who makes a special study of these matters, and knows more about things psychic than any other man in England. The Brands asked me to dinner and arranged to have him also. After dinner he and I went down alone to the doctor's consulting-room, and talked the whole thing out. I was careful to mention no names. You don't want to be credited with a haunted room at the Grange, neither do we want Ronnie's name mixed up with psychical phenomena. Now I will give you this man's opinion and explanation, exactly as he gave it to me. Only, remember, I pass it on as his. I do not necessarily endorse it.

"He holds that inanimate objects, such as beds, walls, cupboards, staircases, have a power of receiving, absorbing and retaining impressions transmitted to them through contact with human minds in extreme conditions of stress and tension. This would especially be the case with intimately personal things, such as musical instruments, or favourite chairs. Old rooms and ancient furniture might retain these impressions for centuries; and, under certain circumstances, transmit them to any mind. with which they came in contact, happening to be strung up to the right key to respond to the psychic impression. He considers that this theory accounts for practically all ghost stories and haunted rooms, passages, and staircases. It reduces all apparitions to the subjective rather than the objective plane; in other words the spirit of a murdered man does not return at certain times to the room in which he was done to death; but his agonised mind, in its last conscious moments, left an impress upon that room which produces a subjective picture of the scene, or part of the scene, upon any mind psychically *en rapport* with that impress. I confess this idea appeals to me. It accounts for the undoubted fact that certain old rooms are undeniably creepy; also that apparitions, unconnected with actual flesh and blood, have been seen by sane and trustworthy witnesses. It does away with the French word for ghost—*revenant*. There is no such thing as a 'comerback,' or an 'earth-bound spirit.' Personally, I do not believe in immortality, in the usually accepted sense of the word; but I have always felt that were there such a thing as a disembodied spirit, it would have something better to do than to walk along old corridors, frightening housemaids! But, to come to the point, concerning our own particular experience.

"I carefully told him every detail. He believes that probably the old Florentine chair and the 'cello had been in conjunction before, and had both played their part in the scene which was re-acted in the mirror. If so, poor old Ron was jolly well in for it, seated in the chair, and holding the 'cello. His already over-excited brain found itself caught between them. The fitful firelight and the large mirror supplied excellent mediums for the visualisation of the subjective picture. Of course, we do not yet know what Ronnie saw. I trust we never shall. It is to be hoped he has forgotten it. Had you and I seen nothing, we should unquestionably have dismissed the whole thing as merely a delirious nightmare of Ronnie's unhinged brain.

"But the undoubted fact remains that we each saw, reflected in that mirror, objects which were not at that moment in the room. In fact we saw the *past* reflected, rather than the *present*. My psychic authority considers that both our impressions came to us through Ronnie's mind, and were already fading, owing to the fact that he had become unconscious. I, coming in later than you, merely saw the Florentine chair in position. All else in my view of the reflection appertained to the actual present, into which the long-ago past was then rapidly merging. But you, coming in a few moments sooner, and being far more *en rapport* with the spirit of the scene, saw the tall man in a red cloak—whom you call the Avenger—strangling the girl. By the way, why do you call him the Avenger?"

"Because," said Helen, slowly, "there was murder in the cruel face of the woman, and there was a dagger in her hand. She had struck her blow before he appeared upon the scene. I know this, because it was the flare of his crimson cloak, as he rushed in, which first caught my eye, in the firelight, and made me look into the mirror at all. Before that I was intent on Ronnie. The Avenger seized the woman from behind; I saw his brown hands on the whiteness of her throat. Grief and horror were on his face, as he looked over her shoulder, and past the chair, at the prostrate heap upon the floor."

"Which heap," said Dick, trying to speak lightly, "was our poor Ronnie."

"No," said Helen, gazing straight before her into the fire; "the heap upon the floor was *not* Ronnie."

"But—I am positive!—I saw it myself! I saw you kneeling beside it. I helped to sort it, afterwards. The actual heap on the floor was the broken chair, Ronnie mixed up with it; and, on top of both, that unholy Infant, whose precocious receptivity is responsible for the entire business. I exonerate the Florentine chair; I exonerate poor Ronnie, I shall always maintain that that confounded 'cello worked the whole show, out of its own unaided tummy!"

But Helen did not laugh. She did not even smile. "The heap on the floor was not Ronnie," she repeated firmly, "nor was I kneeling beside it. The Italian chair had not fallen over. Not a single thing appertaining to the present, was reflected in the picture as I first saw it. Dick, there was a conclusion to my vision of which I have never told you."

"Oh, lor!" said Dick. "When I guaranteed the psychic chap that I was putting him in full possession of every detail!"

"I am sorry, Dick. But until this moment I have never felt able to tell you. I cannot do so now, unless you are nice."

"I *am* nice," said Dick, "*very* nice! Tell me quick."

"Well, as I knelt transfixed, watching—the heap on the floor moved and arose. It was a slight dark man, with a white face, and a mass of tumbled black hair. He lifted from off his breast as he got up, a violoncello. He did not look at the woman, nor at the man in the crimson cloak; he stood staring, as if petrified with grief and dismay, at his 'cello. Following his eyes, I saw a dark jagged stab, piercing its right breast, just above the *f* hole. The anguish on the 'cellist's face, was terrible to see. Then—oh, Dick, I don't know how to tell you!"

"Go on, Helen," he said, gently.

"Then he turned from the 'cello, and looked at *me*; and, Dick, it was the soul of Ronnie—*my* Ronnie—in deepest trouble over his Infant of Prague, which looked at me through those deep sad eyes. I cannot explain to you how I knew it! He was totally unlike my big fair Ronnie, but —it was the soul of Ronnie, in great distress, looking at *me*! The moment I realised this, I seemed set free from the past. The 'cellist, the woman, the Avenger, all vanished instantly. I saw myself reflected, I saw you, I saw the studio; I saw Ronnie on the floor. I turned to him at once, lifted the 'cello from his breast, and drew his head into my lap."

"Was there a jagged hole——"

"No, not a scratch. The stab belonged to a century ago. But, listen, Dick! Several days later, when I had a moment in which to remember Ronnie's poor Infant of Prague, I examined it in a good light, and found the place where the hole made by that dagger had been skillfuly mended."

"Lor!" said Dr. Dick. "We're getting on! Don't you think you and I and the Infant might put our heads together, and write a psychic book! But now—seriously. Do you really believe Ronnie was once a slim, pale person, with a shock of black hair? And if he and his Infant lived together in past ages, where were you and I? Are we altogether out of it? Or are you the lady with the dagger, and I the noble party in the flaming cloak?"

She smiled, and a look of quiet peace was in her eyes.

"Dick," she said. "I am not troubled at all about the past. My whole concern is with the present; my earnest looking forward is to the future. And remember, that which set me completely free to think only of the present, was when my Ronnie's soul looked out at me from that strange vision of the past. I cannot say exactly what I believe. But I know my entire responsibility is to the present; my hope and confidence are towards the future. I realise, as I have never realised before, the deep meaning of the words: 'Lord, Thou hast been our dwelling-place, in all generations.' I am content to leave it at that."

Dick sat silent; sobered, impressed, by a calm confidence of faith, which was new to him.

Then he said: "Good for you, Helen, that you can take it so. Personally, I believe in nothing which I cannot fully explain and understand. 'Faith,' in your sense of the word, has no place in my vocabulary. I was a very small boy when my faith took to itself wings and flew away; and, curiously enough, it was while I was singing lustily, in the village church at Dinglevale: 'As it was in the beginning, is now, and ever shall be: world without end, Amen'!"

"It will come back again," said Helen. "Dick, I know it will come back. Some day you will come to me and you will say: 'It has come back.' The thrusting hand and the prying finger are the fashion nowadays, I know. But the grand old faith which will win out in the end, is the faith which stands with clasped hands, in deepest, reverence of belief; and, lifting adoring eyes, is not ashamed to say to the revelation of a Risen Christ: 'My Lord and my God!' "

Dick stirred uneasily in his chair.

"We have got off the subject," he said. "and it's about time we looked up Ronnie. But, first of all: how much of all this do you mean to tell Ronnie?"

"Nothing whatever, if I can help it," replied Helen. "So far as I know, I hope, after this morning, never to mention the subject again."

"I think you are wise. And now let me give you a

threefold bit of advice. Smash the mirror; burn the chair; brain the Infant!"

Helen laughed. "No, no, Dick!" she said. "I can do none of those things. I must take tenderest care of Ronnie's Infant. I have had his valuable old chair carefully mended; and I must not let him think I fear the mirror."

"You're a brave woman," said Dick. "Believing what you do, you're a brave woman to live in the house with that mirror. Or, perhaps, it comes of believing so much. A certainty of confidence, which asks no questions, must be to some extent a fortifying thing. By the way, you will remember that the long rigmarole I gave you was not my own explanation, but the expert's? Mine is considerably simpler and shorter. In fact, it can be summed up in three words."

"What is your explanation, Dick?"

"Whisky and soda," said Dr. Dick, bravely. "You mixed it stiffer than you knew. I was dead beat, and had had no food. I have always been a fairly abstemious chap; in my profession we have to be: woe betide the man who isn't. But since I saw that chair standing on its four legs in the mirror, when it was lying broken on the floor in reality, I have not touched a drop of alcohol. There! I make you a present of that for your next temperance meeting. Now let's go out and buck Ronnie up. Remember, he'll feel jolly flat for a bit, with no temperature. Temperature is a thing you miss, when it has become a habit."

CHAPTER XVII

"HE NEVER KNEW!"

RONNIE SAW Dick off by the midday train.

After the train had begun to move, Dick leaned from the window, and said suddenly: "Ronnie! talk to your wife about her Leipzig letter, and—*the kid*, you know."

Ronnie kept pace with the train long enough to say: "I wish you wouldn't call it the 'kid,' Dick; it is the 'Infant.' And Helen declines to talk of it."

Then he dropped behind, and Dick flung himself into a corner of his compartment, with a face of comic despair. "Merciful heavens," he said, "slay that Infant!"

Meanwhile Ronnie was saying to a porter: "When is the next train for town?"

"One fifty-five, sir."

"Then I have no chance now of catching the three o'clock from town, for Hollymead?"

"Not from town, sir. But there is a way, by changing twice, which gets you across country, and you pick up the three o'clock all right at Huntingford, four ten."

"Are you sure, my man? I was told there was no way across country."

"The one-fifty-five is the only train in the day by which you can do it, sir. I happen to know, because I have a sister lives at Hollymead, so I've done it m'self. If trains aren't late, you hit off the three o'clock at Huntingford."

"Thanks," said Ronnie, noting down particulars. Then he walked rapidly back to the hotel.

"I can't stand it," he said. "I shall bolt! With me off her hands, she can go and have a jolly Christmas at the Dalmains. She is always welcome there. I must get away alone and think matters out. I know everything is all wrong, and yet I don't exactly know what has come between us. I only know I am wretched, and so is she. It is still the poison of the Upas. If I knew why she suddenly considered me utterly, preposterously, altogether selfish, I would do my level best to put it right. But I don't."

He found Helen in the hall, anxiously watching the door. She took up a paper, as he came in.

"Helen," he said, "do you mind if we lunch punctually at one o'clock? I am going out before two."

"Why, certainly we will," said Helen. "You must have had a very early breakfast, Ronnie. But don't overdo, darling. Remember what Dick said. Shall I come with you?"

"I would rather go alone," said Ronnie. "I want to think things over."

She rose and stood beside him.

"Ronnie dear, we seem to have lost all count of days. But, as a matter of fact, to-morrow is Christmas Day. Would you like to go home this afternoon? We can order a car for two o'clock, and be at the Grange for tea. Ronnie, wouldn't it be rather lovely? Think of the little cosy tea-table, and your own especial chair, and the soft lamplight——"

She paused abruptly. The mental picture had recalled to both the evening on which they last stood together in that golden lamplight.

Ronnie hesitated, looking at the floor. Then he raised his eyes to Helen's. "I don't think I could bear it," he said, turned from her quickly, and went upstairs.

In his room he scribbled a note.

"My wife—I am awfully sorry, but I simply *had* to bolt. Don't be alarmed. I have gone home to the Grange. I believe, when I am by myself in the house where we spent the three years I thought so perfect and so happy, I shall find out what is the matter; I shall get to the very root of the Upas tree.

"I know I somehow hurt you horribly on the night I reached home, by asking you to come to the studio to hear me play my 'cello; but, before God, I haven't the faintest idea why!

"You would not have said what you did had you known I was ill; but neither would you have said it, unless it had been true. If it was true then, it is true now. If it is true now, we can't spend Christmas Day together.

"I want you to go to the Dalmains by motor, as soon as you find this, and have a jolly, restful time with them. You look worn out.

"RONNIE.

"P.S.—I am obliged to leave this in my room. I hope you will find it there. I don't even know where your room is, Helen, in this beastly hotel."

Ronnie considered his postscript; then crossed out "beastly" and substituted "large." But "beastly" still showed, pathetically, beneath the line. And, by and by, the heart of Ronnie's wife, from which all clouds had suddenly rolled away, understood it, and wept over it, and kissed it; and thought "beastly" a dear word! It was so quaintly like Ronnie to substitute "large" for "beastly."

All clouds had rolled away, before Helen read the note; for this is what had happened.

Ronnie had excused himself when lunch was half over.

Helen let him go, trying to act on Dr. Dick's advice not to worry him by seeming to watch or follow him.

So she sat on alone, finishing luncheon, and thus did not see Ronnie walk out of the front door, carrying his bag.

Soon afterwards she passed into the hall, and sat dipping into the papers and thinking over her talk with Dick.

Presently a page stepped up to her with a letter, on a salver.

Her heart stood still as she saw the stamp, the postmark, and the writing. It was from Aubrey Treherne, forwarded from Hollymead.

Helen was sorely tempted for a moment to burn it unread. She had suffered so much through a former letter in that handwriting. She suddenly realised how cruelly Aubrey's words about Ronnie had, in the light of Ronnie's subsequent behaviour, eaten into her soul.

She looked at the fire. She rose and moved towards it, the letter in her hand.

Then better counsels prevailed.

She went slowly upstairs to her sitting-room, closed the door, sat down, and opened Aubrey's letter.

It contained a smaller envelope sealed, on which was written: "Read letter first."

She opened the folded sheets.

"DEAR HELEN,

"Yes, you are right about God's Word not returning void. Your own words, I admit, only hardened me; but those at the end of your letter broke me up. I am so very far removed from light and fellowship, love and forgiveness. I doubt if I can ever get back into the way of peace.

"But, anyhow, before the great Feast of Peace upon earth, goodwill toward men, I can take a first step by fully confessing the great wrong I did to you and to your husband rather more than a month ago, on the evening which he spent at my flat.

"Possibly you have found it out already; but possibly not, as I hear he has been very seriously ill.

"The evening he was here, he was more or less queer and light-headed, but he was full of you, and of his delight in going home. I suppose this all helped to madden me. No need to explain why. You know.

"He had found a letter from you at the *Poste Restante*; but, rushing around to his publishers, etc., had not had time to read it.

"When he remembered it and found it in his pocket-book, he stood with his back to my stove, in great excitement, and tore it open; I sitting by.

"As he unfolded the large sheets of foreign paper, a note flew out from between them, and fell, unseen by him, to the floor.

"I put my foot on it. I gathered, from extracts he read me from the letter, that this note was of importance.

"When he found in a postscript that you mentioned an enclosure, he hunted everywhere for it; not thinking, of course, to look under my foot.

"He then concluded, on my instigation, that, after all, you had not enclosed any note.

"At the first opportunity I transferred it to my pocket, made an excuse to leave the room, and read it.

"Helen, believe me, had I known beforehand the news that note contained, I don't think I could have been such a fiend.

"But once having done it, I carried it through. I allowed your husband to go home in total ignorance of the birth of his son. It was I who put the word 'astonishing' into his telegram; and, in my letter to you, I led you to suppose I had heard the news from him.

"I don't know exactly what I expected to gain from all this. But, in a condition of mad despair, I seemed playing my very last card; and I played it for all it was worth—which apparently was not much!

"I did plenty of other devilish work that night—chiefly mental suggestion. This is the only really confessable thing.

"The letter your husband never saw, is in the enclosed envelope. He will like to have it now.

"Thus, as you see, the Word has not returned unto you void. It brings you the only reparation I can make.

"AUBREY TREHERNE."

Helen tore open the sealed envelope, and found her little pencil note, the tender outpouring to Ronnie, written three days after her baby's birth.

So Ronnie never saw it—he never knew! He came home without having the remotest idea that she had been through anything unusual in his absence. He had heard no word or hint of the birth of his little son. Yet she had called him utterly, preposterously, altogether selfish, because he had quite naturally expected her to be as interested as ever in his pursuits and pleasures.

Oh, Ronnie, Ronnie!

She flew to his room, hoping he had not yet gone out. On the table she found a note addressed to herself.

She tore it open, read it—then went back into the sitting-room, and pealed the bell.

"Send my maid to me at once, and the hall-porter."

They arrived together.

Helen had just written a long telegram to her house-keeper.

She spoke to the hall-porter first.

"Send off this telegram, please. Then procure the fastest motor-car you can find, to run me over to Hollymead this afternoon. We can be ready to start in half-an-hour's time."

Then she turned to her maid.

"Jeffreys, we go home for Christmas after all. Mr. West has gone on by train. We must pack as promptly as possible, and start in half an hour. We may perhaps get home before him. I doubt whether he can catch anything down from town before the five o'clock."

She flew to her room, pressing Ronnie's sad little note to her heart. All the world looked different! Ah, what would it be, now, to tell him of his little son! But she must get home before him. Supposing Ronnie went upstairs alone, and found the baby!

CHAPTER XVIII

THE FACE IN THE MIRROR

RONNIE CAUGHT the three o'clock train from town, at Huntingford, as the porter had predicted.

No carriage was at the station, so he had a rather long walk from Hollymead to the Grange.

It was a clear, crisp evening and freezing hard. He could feel the frost crackle under his feet, as he tramped along the country lanes.

When he came in sight of the lodge, it reminded him of an old-fashioned Christmas card; the large iron gates, their grey stone supports covered with moss and lichen and surmounted by queer rampant beasts unknown to zoology, holding in their stone claws oval shields on which were carved the ancient arms of Helen's family; the little ivy-covered house, with gabled roof and lattice-windows, firelight from within, shining golden and ruddy on the slight sprinkling of frosty snow.

As he passed in at the gate he saw the motherly figure of Mrs. Simpkins, a baby on her arm, appear at the window, lifting her hand to draw down the crimson blind. Before the blind shut in the bright interior, Ronnie caught a glimpse of three curly heads round a small Christmas tree on the kitchen-table. Simpkins, in his shirt-sleeves, was lighting the topmost candle.

Ronnie walked on beneath the chestnuts and beeches, up the long sweep of the park drive, a dark lonely figure.

He was very tired; his heart was heavy and sad.

It had been such a cheery glimpse of home, through the lodge window, before the red blind shut it in. Simpkins was a lucky fellow. Mrs. Simpkins looked so kind and comfortable, with the baby's head nestling against her capacious bosom.

Ronnie turned to look back at the brightly lighted cottage. The ruddy glow from the blind, fell on the snow. He wondered whether there was a Upas tree in that humble home. Surely not! A Upas tree and a Christmas-tree could hardly find place in the same home. The tree of Light and Love, would displace the tree of subtle poison.

He turned wearily from the distant light and plodded on.

Then he remembered that, in her last letter, Helen had said: "Ronnie, we will have a Christmas tree this Christmas." Why had Helen said that? He had fully intended to ask her, but had not thought of it from that hour to this.

Possibly it was just a wish to yield to his whim in the matter. Perhaps she was planning to have all the little Simpkins kids up to the house.

Well, if Helen spent Christmas with the Dalmains, she would come in for little Geoff's Christmas tree, which would certainly be a beauty.

He plodded heavily on. He felt extraordinarily lonely. Would Helen miss him? Hardly. You do not miss a selfish person. He would miss Helen—horribly; but then Helen was not selfish. She was quite the most unselfish person he had ever known.

He went over in his mind all the times when Helen had instantly given up a thing at his wish. Amongst others, he remembered how, on that spring morning so long ago, when he had told her of his new book and of his plan, she had been wanting to tell him something, yet he had allowed her interest to remain untold, when she threw herself heart and soul into his. He began to wonder what it could have been; and whether it would be too late to ask her now.

At last he reached the house, and felt slightly cheered to see lights and fires within. He had almost anticipated darkness.

Mrs. Blake herself opened the door, resplendent in black satin; lavender ribbons in her lace cap.

"La, sir!" she said. "Fancy you walking from the station! You must please to excuse Simpkins being out. He has some Christmasing on at the lodge, for his fam'ly."

"I know," said Ronnie. "I saw a Christmas tree as I passed. I shall not require Simpkins. Blake, is there a fire in the studio?"

"There is, sir, a fine one, for the good of the piano. There is also a fire in the sitting-room, sir, where I will at once send in some tea."

"No, not there," said Ronnie quickly. "I will have tea in the studio."

But Mrs. Blake was firm. "That I couldn't ever, sir. Mrs. West wouldn't wish it. She thinks so much of you having tea in her sitting-room, and beside her fire; which is much more, so to say, cosy than that great unfurnished room, all looking-glass."

At mention of the mirror Ronnie shivered, and yielded. He had almost forgotten the mirror.

So he sat in his own favourite chair, while Blake stood and poured out his first cup of tea, then left him to the utter loneliness of being in that room without Helen.

It is doubtful whether Ronnie had ever loved his wife so passionately as he loved her while he experienced, for the first time, what it was like to be without her, in the room where they had hitherto always been together.

Everything he touched, everything at which he looked, spoke of Helen; forcing upon him the consciousness of the sweetness of her presence, and the consequent hardness of her absence.

Yet he had brought this hardness on himself. She had said: "Wouldn't it be rather lovely to have tea together?" But he had answered: "I don't think I could bear it." And now he did not know how to bear the fact that she was not with him.

Then he saw the chair against which he had leaned his

'cello, and with a thrill of comfort he remembered the Infant of Prague.

How had it fared all this time, in its canvas bag? Perhaps no one had remembered even to put it back into that.

Having hastily swallowed his tea, lest Blake should arrive at the studio to inquire what had been amiss with it, Ronnie hurried down the corridor, entered the long, low room, and turned on the electric light. As before, a great log fire burned on the hearth; but he needed more light now, than mere fitful fire-gleams. He wanted to examine the Infant.

He looked round the room, and there, on a wide settee under one of the windows, lay a polished, rosewood 'cello-case.

Ronnie, springing forward, bent down eagerly. The key was in the lock. He turned it, and lifted the lid.

There lay the Infant, shining and beautiful as ever, in a perfectly-fitting bed, lined with soft white velvet. The whole thing carried out exactly Ronnie's favourite description of his 'cello: "just like the darkest horse-chestnut you ever saw in a bursting bur." The open rosewood case, with its soft white lining, was the bursting bur; and within lay his beautiful Infant!

Helen had done this.

Ronnie's pleasure was largely tinged with pain. Helen, who did not like his 'cello, had done this to please him, yet was not here to see his pleasure.

Ronnie drew forth the bow from its place in the lid, opened a little nest which held the rosin, then tenderly lifted the Infant of Prague and carried it to the light.

At first sight, its shining surface appeared perfect as ever. Then, looking very closely, and knowing exactly where to look, Ronnie saw a place just above the _f_ hole on the right, where a blow had evidently been struck deeply into the 'cello. A strip of wood, four inches long, by one

inch wide, had been let in, then varnished so perfectly
that the mend—probably the work of a hundred years ago
—could only be seen in a good light, and *by one who knew
exactly where to look.*

Ronnie stood with grave face gazing at the Infant.

What did it all mean?

He remembered with the utmost vividness every detail
of the scene in the mirror.

Had he thought-read from his 'cello the happenings of
a century before? Had it transmitted to his overwrought
brain, the scene in which it had once played so prominent
a part?

Had it, before then, in the Leipzig flat, imparted to
Aubrey Treherne—unconsciously to himself—an accurate
mental picture of its former owner?

Ronnie mused on this, and wondered. Then the desire
rose strong within him to hear once more the golden voice
of the Infant, even at the risk of calling up again those
ghostly phantoms of a vanished past.

He drew the Florentine chair into the centre of the room.

He took his seat on the embossed leather of crimson and
gold.

He glanced at his reflection. His face was whiter than it
had been five weeks ago, when he returned, deep bronzed,
from Africa. His hair, too, was longer than it ought to be;
though not so long as the heavy black locks of the 'cellist
of that past reflection.

Ronnie's rough tweed suit and shooting-boots, were a
curious contrast to the satin knee-breeches, silken hose, and
diamond shoe-buckles he remembered in his vision; yet
his manner of holding the 'cello, assumed without conscious
thought, and the positions of his knees and feet, were so
precisely those of that quaint old-time figure, that Ronnie
never doubted that when he raised the bow and his fingers
bit into the strings, the flood of harmony would be the same.

He waited for the strong tremor to seize his wrist.

It did not come.

He sounded the four open strings, slowly, one after the other.

Yes, the tones were very pure, very rich, very clear.

Then he took courage, pressed his finger into the finger-board, and began to play.

Alas, poor Infant of Prague!

Alas, poor *born* musician, who preferred doing things he had never learned to do!

The exquisite rise and fall of harmony, came not again.

Bitterly disappointed, Ronnie waited, staring into the mirror.

But a rather weary, very lonely, and exceedingly modern young man stared back at him.

At last he realised that he could no longer play the 'cello by inspiration. So he began very carefully feeling for the notes.

The Infant squeaked occasionally, and wailed a little; but on the whole it behaved very well; and, after half-an-hour's work, having found out the key which enabled him to use chiefly the open strings, Ronnie managed to play right through, very fairly in tune, "O come, all ye faithful, joyful and triumphant!"

This gave him extraordinary pleasure. It seemed such a certainty of possession, to be able to pick out all the notes for himself.

He longed that Helen might be there to hear.

The Infant of Prague grew dearer to him than ever. He was now mastering it himself, independent of the antics of an old person of a century ago, bowing away in the mirror.

He tried again; and this time he sang the words of the first verse, as he played. His really fine baritone blended well with the richness of the silver strings.

The words had occasionally to wait, suspended as it were in mid-air, while he felt about wildly for the note on the 'cello; but, once found, the note was true and good, and likely to lead more or less easily to the next.

A listener, in the corridor outside, pressed her hands to her breast, uncertain whether she felt the more inclined to laugh or to weep.

Ronnie began his verse again.

"O come . . . all ye . . . faithful . . . joyful and tri . . . tri . . . tri . . . *um* . . . phant . . . O come, ye, O come ye, to Beth . . . Beth . . . Beth . . . Be—eth—le—*hem*!"

He paused, exhausted by the effort of drawing Bethlehem complete, out of the complication of the Infant's four vibrating strings.

He paused, and, lifting his eyes, looked into the mirror—and saw therein the face of a woman, watching him from beside the door; a lovely face, all smiles, and tears, and tenderness.

At first he gazed, unable to believe his eyes. But, when her eyes met his, and she knew that he saw her, she moved quickly forward, kneeled down beside him, and—it was the face of his wife, all flooded with glad tenderness, which, resting against his shoulder, looked up into his.

She had spoken no word; yet at the first sight of her Ronnie knew that the cloud which had been between them, was between no longer.

"Helen," he said; "Oh, Helen!"

CHAPTER XIX

UNTO US A CHILD IS BORN

RONNIE LAID down his bow, and put his right arm round his wife.

He still held the precious Infant of Prague between his knees, his left hand on the ebony finger-board.

"My darling!" Helen said. "So we shall be at home for Christmas after all. How glad I am!"

He looked at her dumbly, and waited.

He felt like the prodigal, who had planned to suggest as his only possible desert, a place among the hired servants, but was so lifted into realisation of sonship by the father's welcome, that perforce he left that sentence unspoken.

So Ronnie looked at her dumbly, reading the utter love for him in her eyes.

Back came the words of his hymn, replete with fresh meaning.

> "O come, all ye faithful,
> Joyful and triumphant!"

They were such faithful eyes—Helen's; and now they seemed filled with triumphant joy.

"Ronnie," she said, "do you remember how I wrote to you at Leipzig, that this Christmas we would have a Christmas tree? Did not you wonder, darling, why I said that?"

"Yes," answered Ronnie. "I thought of it this evening when I saw a Christmas tree at the lodge. I had meant to ask you the night I reached home, but I did not remember then."

"Ah, if you had," she said, "if you only had!'"

"Well?" he questioned. "Tell me now."

"Ronnie, do you remember that in that letter I said I had something to tell you, and that I enclosed a note, written some weeks before, telling you this thing?"

"Yes, dear," said Ronnie. "But you forgot to enclose the note. It was not there. I tore the envelope right open; I hunted high and low. Then we concluded you had after all considered it unimportant."

"It was all-important, Ronnie; and it *was* there."

"It was—*where?*" asked Ronnie.

"Under Aubrey's foot. . . . Oh, hush, darling, hush! We must not say hard things of a man who has confessed, and who is bitterly repentant. I can't tell you the whole story now; you shall hear every detail later; but he saw it fall from the letter, as you opened it. He was tempted, first, to cover it with his foot; then, to put it in his pocket; and, after he had read it, he wrote to me implying that you had told him the news it contained; so, when you arrived home, how could I possibly imagine that you did not know it?"

"Did not know *what*?" asked Ronnie.

She drew a folded paper from her pocket.

"My darling, this will tell you best. It is the note intended to reach you at Leipzig; it is the note which, until this afternoon, I had all along believed you to have received."

She put her note into his hand.

"I hope you will be able to read it by this light, Ronnie. I was very weak when I wrote it. I could only use pencil."

Ronnie unfolded it gravely.

She knelt, with bowed head, beside him. She dared not watch his face.

She heard his breath come short and fast. He moved his knees, and let go his 'cello.

The Infant of Prague slipped unnoticed to the floor.

When he read of the birth of his little son, with a hard choking sob, Ronnie turned and gathered her to him, holding her close, yet eagerly reading the letter over her head; reading it, to its very last word.

Then, dropping the letter, he clasped her to him, with a strength and a depth of tenderness such as she had never before known in Ronnie. And his first words were not what Helen had expected.

"Helen," he said, with another desperate tearless sob, "oh, to think that you had to go through *that*—alone!"

"My darling boy," she answered, "don't worry about that! It is all over, now; and it is so true—oh, *so* true, Ronnie—that the anguish is no more remembered in the greatness of the joy."

"But I can't forget," said Ronnie—"I shall never forget
—that my wife bore the suffering, the danger, the weakness,
and I was not there to share it. I did not even know what
she was going through."

"Ronnie dear—think of your little son."

"I can think of nothing of mine just yet," he answered,
"excepting of my wife."

She gave in to his mood, and waited; letting him hold
her close in perfect silence.

It was strangely sweet to Helen, because it was so completely unexpected. She had been prepared for a moment of
intense surprise, followed by a rapture of pride and delight;
then a wild rush to the nursery to see his first-born. She
was quite willing, now her part was over, that her part should
be forgotten. It was as unexpected as it was comfortingly
precious, that Ronnie should be thus stricken by the thought
of her pain, and of her need of him to help her bear it.

At last he said: "Helen, I see it all now. It was the Upas
tree indeed: utterly, preposterously, altogether selfish!"

"My darling, no!" she cried. "Oh, don't be so unjust to
yourself! When I used those terrible words, I thought you
had had my letter, had come home knowing it all, yet
absorbed completely in other things. Misled by Aubrey,
I cruelly misjudged you, Ronnie. It was not selfish to go;
it was not selfish to be away. You did not know, or you
would not have gone. I was glad you should not know,
glad you should be away, so that I could bear it alone,
without hindering your work; letting you find the joy when
you reached home, without having had any of the hardness
or the worry. I wished it to be so, my darling boy—and I
was glad."

Then Ronnie gently put his wife out of his arms, and
took her sweet face between his hands, looking long into
her eyes, before he made reply. And Helen, steadfastly
returning his gaze, saw a look growing in her husband's

face, such as she had never yet seen there, and knew, even before he began to speak, what he was going to say; and her protective love, longing as ever to shield him from pain, cried out: "Oh, must I let him realise that?"

But, at last, through the guidance of wiser Hands than hers, the matter had passed beyond Helen's control.

"My wife," said Ronnie slowly, "when I called it 'the Upas tree indeed,' I did not mean the *one* act of going off in ignorance and leaving you alone during the whole of that time, when any man who cared at all would wish to be at hand, to bear, and share, and guard. I do not brand that as selfish; because you purposely withheld from me the truth, and bid me go. But *why* did you withhold it? Why, after the first shock, did you feel glad to face the prospect of bearing it alone; glad I should be away? Ah, here we find the very roots of the Upas tree! Was it not because, during the whole of our married life, I have been cheerfully, complacently selfish? I have calmly accepted as the rule of the home, that I should hear of no worries which you could keep from me, tread upon no thorns which you could clear out of my path, bear no burdens which your loving hands could lift and carry out of sight. Your interests, your pleasures, your friends, your pursuits, all have been swept on one side, if they seemed in the smallest degree likely to interfere with my work, my desires, my career. You have lived for me—absolutely. I have lived for myself. True, we have loved each other tenderly; we have been immensely happy. But, all the while, the shadow of the Upas tree was there. My very love was selfish! It was sheer joy to love you, because you are so sweetly, so altogether, lovable. But when did I—because of my love for you—do one single thing at any cost to self? I was utterly, preposterously, altogether selfish! You knew this. You knew I hated pain, or worry, or anything which put my comfortable life out of gear. So you gladly let me go, leaving you to bear it all alone. You knew that, had you told me, I should have given up my book and stayed with you; because my self-love would have been more wounded by going than by staying. But you also knew that during all those months you would have had to listen while I bemoaned the circumstances, and bewailed my plot. You knew the bloom would be taken off the coming joy, so you preferred to let me go. Oh, Helen, is not this true?"

She bent her head and kissed his hand. She was weeping silently. She could not say it was not true.

"It was the Upas tree indeed," said Ronnie.

"Darling," she whispered, "it was my fault too——"

"Hush," he said. "There are faults too noble to be accounted faults. But—if you think you were at all to blame—you must atone, by truly and faithfully helping in my fight to root up the Upas tree."

"Ronnie," she said, "a pair of baby hands will help us both. We must learn to live life at its highest, for the sake of our little son."

Then, knowing he had endured as much heart-searching as a man could bear and be the better for it, she said, smiling:

"Ronnie, his funny little hands are so absurdly like yours."

"Like *mine*?" repeated Ronnie, as one awakening slowly from a sad dream, to a blissful reality. "Why are they like mine?"

"Because he is a tiny miniature of you, you dear, silly old boy! You do not seem to understand that you are actually a father, Ronnie, with a little son of your own!"

She looked up into his worn face, and saw the young glad joy of life creep slowly back into it.

"And his mouth, darling—his little mouth is just like yours; only, as I told you in the letter, when I kiss it—it does not kiss back, Ronnie."

"What?" cried Ronnie. "What?"

Then he understood; and, this time, it was no mirage. Ronnie's desert wanderings were over.

"But don't you want to see your son?" Helen asked, presently.

Ronnie leapt up.

"See him? Why, of course I do! Oh come on! . . . Helen! What does one say to a very young baby?"

Helen followed him upstairs, laughing.

"That entirely depends upon circumstances. One usually says: 'Did it?' 'Is it then?' or 'Was it?' But I almost think present conditions require a more definite statement of fact. I fancy one would say: 'How do you do, baby? *I* am your papa!' . . . This way, Ronnie, in my own old nurseries. Oh, darling, I am afraid I am going to cry! But you must not mind. They will only be tears of unutterable joy. Think what it will be to me, to see my baby in his father's arms!"

CHAPTER XX

GOOD-NIGHT TO THE INFANT OF PRAGUE

THE LAST hour of Christmas Eve ticked slowly to its close.

On all around grew that sense of the herald angels, bending over a waiting world, poised upon outstretched wings. The hush had fallen which carries the mind away to the purple hills of Bethlehem, the watching shepherds, the quiet folds, the sudden glory in the sky.

The old Grange was closing its eyes at last, and settling itself to slumber.

One by one the brightly lighted windows darkened; the few remaining lights moved upwards.

The Hollymead waits had duly arrived, and played their annual Christmas hymns. They had won gold from Ronnie, by ministering to his new-found proud delight in his infant son. The village blacksmith, who played the cornet and also acted spokesman for the band, had closed the selections of angelic music, by exclaiming hoarsely, under cover of the night: "A merry Christmas and a 'appy New Year, to Mrs. West, to Mr. West, and to *Master* West!"

Ronnie dashed out jubilant. The waits departed well-content.

Helen said: "You dear old silly!"

"Master West," wakened by the cornet, also had something to say; but he confided his remarks to his nurse, and was soon hushed back to slumber.

.   .   .   .   .

In the studio, the fire burned low.

The reflections in the long mirror, were indefinite and dim.

The Infant of Prague lay forgotten on the floor.

.   .   .   .   .

As midnight drew very near, the door of the studio was pushed softly open, and Helen came in, wearing a soft white wrapper; a lighted candle in her hand.

She placed the candle on a table; then, stooping, carefully lifted Ronnie's 'cello from the floor, laid it in its rosewood case, and stood looking down upon it. Then, smiling, touched its silver strings, with loving fingers.

"Poor Infant of Prague!" she said. "Has Ronnie forgotten even to put you to bed? Never mind! To-morrow you and he shall sing Christmas hymns together, while I and his little son listen and admire."

She closed the case. Then some impulse made her open it again. Her sweet eyes filled with tears. No one was there to see. Ronnie's wife knelt down and gently kissed the unconscious, shining face of the Infant of Prague.

.   .   .   .   .   .

Turning from the settee beneath the window, she saw herself reflected in the mirror—a tall fair figure in trailing garments, soft and white.

She held the candle high above her head, looked at her own reflection, and smiled.

She was glad she was so lovely—for Ronnie's sake.

Ronnie's love to-night was very wonderful.

She moved towards the door, but paused in passing to look into the smouldering embers of the fire.

At that moment the clocks struck midnight. She heard the Westminster chimes, up on the landing.

It was Christmas Day.

"Unto us a Child is born; unto us a Son is given," murmured Helen. "Oh, holy Christ of Christmas, may the new life to come be very perfect for my Ronnie, my baby, and me!"

.   .   .   .   .   .

"Helen!" came Ronnie's eager happy voice, shouting over the stairs. "I say, *Helen!* Where are you?"

"Coming, darling!" she called, passing out of the studio, and moving swiftly down the corridor.

Ronnie, on the landing, was leaning over the banisters, an expression of comic dismay on his face.

"Oh, I say!" he whispered. "I've done it now! I believe I've woke the baby!"

Helen, mounting the stairs, paused to look up at him, love and laughter in her eyes.

"Undoubtedly you have, you naughty boy! No shouting allowed here now, after dark. But what do you think I was doing? Why, I was in the studio, putting to bed the Infant of Prague."